The Forest

Justin Groot

/ / /

For Opa

ACKNOWLEDGMENTS

This book would never have happened if not for the endless support and encouragement I received from Ginny C, my parents, and the subscribers of r/FormerFutureAuthor.

Thank you.

When was the first time you saw the forest?

I was nine. A dense fog had descended on New England, where my family was spending an impromptu vacation, but we persevered, loaded up the car and drove out early to beat the crowds. Headlights slipped through the murk like phosphorescent eyes. My father hunched over the wheel, muttering more than usual. My mother had been gone for sixteen months. In the back seat, I held my little brother's hand.

We parked near the coast and climbed the trail to a lighthouse on the cliffs.

Television had not prepared me for the view. Fog boiled away into treetops without end. Green canopy unfolded all the way to the horizon. A bird cried out and was answered. Wind snickered through the leaves. In the distance, at the very limit of my vision, something huge began to move.

1

Date: Tue, 29 Mar 2017 15:11:45 -0800 (PST)
From: L. Alvarez
Subject: Re: More preposterous claims
emanating from your department
To: T. Porter

Since giving the Senator another geology lesson strikes this public servant as an egregious misuse of time and tax dollars, she would kindly direct the Senator to an informative video, available on various streaming services, wherein Neil deGrasse Tyson traipses across a tremendous calendar, pontificating at tedious length on what humanity's twelve thousand years amount to, on a geologic scale, which (spoiler) is nothing. Should the Senator continue, after watching this video, to feel the need to harass this public servant with his laughable belief that things on Earth have always been precisely as they exist today – let alone to continue addressing her as "young lady" - he is kindly invited to fuck a lawn mower.

After nine months, Sergeant Rivers decided it was time for our first expedition. He split us into trios. I expected him to group me with Zip and Lindsey Li, since the three of us spent most of our time together, but instead I wound up with Sam Vazquez Jr. and Hollywood.

I didn't mind Junior. Hollywood was another matter.

"Put me in Li's group," I said.

Sergeant Rivers was seven feet tall, and he moved with the slow precision of someone who'd spent a lifetime accidentally smashing objects in his vicinity.

"Excuse me?" he said.

"Look, Tetris," said Hollywood, "we know you'll miss your little girlfriend out there, but if you really can't go four days without a blow job, I'm sure Junior will fill in."

I took a step. Zip grabbed my shoulder, but it wasn't me Hollywood needed to worry about. Li's current expression typically preceded somebody's nose being broken by about fifteen seconds.

"Next recruit to dispute an order packs their bags," roared Rivers. "I've got nipple hairs that mean more to me than you do."

He directed a cycloptic glare at each of us, the mess of interlocking scar tissue in his empty left eye socket crumpling horribly.

"As for you," he said, turning to Hollywood, "keep your god damn mouth shut."

I was pissed all day. So was Li.

"I don't know what you've been telling people, Tetris," she said, right before we turned in for the night, "but we're just friends. I'd never date you in a million years."

Hollywood, three bunks over, let out a hoot.

So then I couldn't even fall asleep. Not that I was into Li. I was just trying to figure out what was so wrong with me, that she'd say something like that.

When I woke up, it felt like someone had crammed cotton balls into the space behind my eyes. The hour-long ride to the coast passed in a hazy blur. Each time I slipped into sleep, my head tipped forward, waking me up again.

At the Coast Guard checkpoint, a bleary-eyed guardsman lifted himself out of his chair and came to check our credentials. A helicopter puttered overhead, following a row of concrete towers that receded down the coast like the pylons of some long-crumbled bridge. Rivers expelled us at the forest's edge and drove away without a word.

It was cool enough that I didn't want to stand still, so I shuffled my feet on the dewy grass. The sun sat fat and low behind us, sending rays of light that pelted into the forest and scattered. Trees like cathedral columns stretched into dim infinity. Their bases were obscured by plants that clawed over one another, battling for whatever scraps of sunlight made it through. Tapestries of moss hung from low branches and rugged contours of bark.

A distant creature made a sound like water drops in a deep bucket. Others crooned and squealed and sang. We waited for a while, but nothing showed itself. Only the canopy moved, shifting veils of brilliant green.

Hollywood rocked on his heels, drawing air through

flared nostrils. His blond hair was just short of the insubordinate length at which Rivers would order it all shaved off.

"Finally," he said, and headed down the slope.

Rangers only brought one assault rifle on expeditions, typically a SCAR-17, since it was more important to pack light than to be heavily armed. Naturally, Hollywood had demanded to carry our rifle. He led the way through the forest with springy, cheerful steps. Junior and I grimaced behind him. At least this wouldn't take very long. Two days in and two days back: a fraction the length of a normal expedition.

My personal mission was to grit my teeth and avoid getting in a fight. Maybe, if this went well, Rivers would put me in a different group next time. The whole thing was probably an attempt to teach me a lesson about working with people I didn't like, which, frankly, was a lesson Rivers could stuff right between his sickeningly well-defined glutes.

For a long while it was silent and still. A few hours passed. We kept our eyes on the ground, avoiding colorful plants and scum-rimmed puddles, as we worked our way between the enormous trees. Right when I'd begun to wonder if the entire day would pass uneventfully, branches just out of sight began to snap, and we took cover in a bank of ferns. Something went crunching by, obscured by a tangle of vines and foliage. Red-brown bulk and rippling muscle showed through the gaps. Whatever it was, it was big, especially for this close to shore. Blood thumped in my ears. The gear I'd grown used to carrying in training—backpack, sidearm, grapple gun, body cameras—suddenly felt unwieldy and conspicuous. I held my breath and glanced at the others.

Hollywood was smiling. I wanted to elbow him in his bright white teeth.

When we could no longer hear the creature's passage through the reeds, we continued on our way. By noon we were further into the forest than I'd ever been. Green-gold motes of pollen or dust drifted in the air, glittering when they crossed columns of sunlight. The trees here made the ones by the coast look like saplings. We'd passed the edge of the continental shelf, where the earth sloped sharply downward and the forest rose to take its place. Everywhere around us, there were cave-ins, green ravines leading into darkness. Five hundred feet down, you'd find the loamy remains of trees that predated the pyramids.

My head began to throb. A thumb-sized horsefly landed on my arm and popped like a grape when I swatted it.

Ninety-eight percent of the sun's light is blocked by the canopy. Because there's hardly any light to work with, shadows are hard to spot. If I hadn't happened to glance up at the right moment, I wouldn't have noticed the carpet snake gliding down on its broad, wing-like rib cage until it was far too late.

"Incoming," I shouted, drawing my pistol. The creature's twenty-foot wingspan billowed at the edges. I opened fire. Each hit created an sputtering fountain of black blood. The crescent mouth gaped stupidly. Fangs shone white and sharp inside.

As the carpet snake crumpled and fell, its tender underbelly ruptured, I slammed a new magazine into the pistol. Hollywood and Junior were already arming their grapple guns. Gunshots drew attention. We'd have to lie low for a while.

"Nice eye," said Junior when we were safe on a branch high above.

I didn't trust my shivering lips to respond.

When the forest seemed to have forgotten we were there, we rappelled down and went to look at the creature's body. It was gone. Something had dragged it into a nearby ravine, leaving a trail of squashed vegetation the width of a snow plow.

"How much you think that thing weighed?" asked Junior.

"Five hundred pounds, easy," said Hollywood. He blew a bright pink bubble.

I squinted at him. "You brought gum out here?"

The bubble, baseball-sized, popped. "Got a problem?"

I shrugged, remembering my mission.

We took it slow. Thickets of curled pink flowers lined our path. The flowers gave off an odor of rotting flesh, drawing clouds of curious flies.

In some places the trees grew so thick together that they became a maze with towering bark-lined walls. Most of the time, there was a moist, earthy aroma, like the smell in the woods back home after it rained. But then there were spots that smelled even worse than the pink flowers. When you came across one of those, you hustled through. You hoped the odor originated from a rotting carcass, because the living things that smelled like that were uniformly horrifying.

We'd just exited one of those awful-smelling areas when we called it a day. Darkness would be falling soon, and we wanted to be up in the branches before then, tucked away in our camouflaged sleeping bags.

I only managed two hours of sleep that first night. Nothing had prepared me for the barrage of sounds. I held my breath after every rustle and screech. My eyes strained to pierce the sludge at the aperture of the sleeping bag, but as hard as I pushed against it, the darkness pushed back harder.

Surely the monsters could hear me breathing from the forest floor. When the jaws closed around my skull, would I have time to feel the pain, or would my death come quicker than my nerves could sense it? I braced myself and hoped for the latter.

In the morning, purple bags lurked below Junior's bloodshot eyes. I must have had those too. My muscles and tendons were gritty with sleep deprivation, and my head pounded. Thinking about the length of the day ahead made me physically ill.

Hollywood looked like he'd scored ten hours on a fluffy king bed. He chattered all through breakfast. As we lowered ourselves to the forest floor, I actually heard him whistling—whistling!—until something out of sight unleashed a mucousy roar. That shut him up.

A few hours of walking later, I ducked behind a tree to relieve myself and came face-to-face with an enormous brown insect, its mouth yawning in a toothless grin. I leapt back, but the bug didn't move. After a moment I realized the eye sockets were empty. It was a gigantic version of the exoskeletons that dotted the trees in my back yard every fall.

I must have yelled, because Junior poked his head around the corner.

"Well, that's horrifying," he said.

I prodded the husk with a finger. It was thicker than I'd thought, and tough, like fiberglass.

"In Baltimore we get a big cicada swarm every seventeen years," said Junior. "Last one was in 2013. Sky turned black. You'd step on them everywhere. The smell was awful."

Hollywood came to have a look.

"Neat," he said. He leveled the SCAR at the exoskeleton and fired off a burst.

The gunfire was impossibly loud. Junior's nostrils doubled in size. He picked Hollywood up by his pack straps. "Are you insane?"

Junior was almost as big as Rivers. Definitely not a guy you wanted to fuck with. Two months ago, when Scott Brown decided he'd had enough and tried to stab Hollywood with a knife from the kitchen, it had been Junior who stepped in and hurled the would-be-assassin through a wall.

Hollywood slithered out of the pack and danced away. "Was curious if these were bulletproof," he said, sticking a finger through one of the neat round holes. "Looks like they're not."

"I'm going to murder you," hissed Junior. He threw the pack at Hollywood, nearly knocking him down. I searched the canopy for movement. The forest crashed and rumbled, awakened from its slumber.

"Relax. We'll hit the branches and wait it out."

"Not an option," I said, stomach flattening, as a tarantula the size of a bus broke through the leaves and skittered down a trunk toward us.

We ran. Hollywood, out front, hefted the SCAR in both hands and leapt a fallen branch. Junior and I could barely keep up. We tore through a dense patch of vegetation and across a porous section of forest floor, weaving between pits with hungry black gullets.

Up ahead, a flesh wasp hovered, swollen stinger twitching in the air. Hollywood led us left. The flesh wasp buzzed after us. The giant insect's sting carried an overpowering paralytic venom, but the awful part was that it also injected a larva. After stinging you, the wasp would continue on its way, but your misery would only have begun: in the days that followed, the larva would devour you from the inside, assuming something didn't find you lying there first.

Soon our path was blocked again, this time by a fleet of blimp-sized jellyfish. Filled with hydrogen gas, the jellyfish wobbled gently off of tree trunks and each other as they floated through the forest. Curtains of silvery tentacles draped beneath them, dredging for warm-blooded prey.

The jellyfish blocked every direction except the one we'd come from, and they were drifting steadily toward us.

I spun and found the tarantula clambering into view. Its legs were the diameter of telephone poles. The flesh wasp was nowhere to be seen.

"Junior," I said, "you've got incendiary rounds, right?"

"Yeah," said Junior.

"In your pistol?"

"Yeah."

"Give it to me."

He handed it over. The tarantula observed, frozen except for its fidgeting mouthparts, as the wall of tentacles rustled closer.

"When I fire," I said, "run straight at the spider."

Junior opened his mouth, but I held up a hand.

"Hollywood," I said, "Hit it in the eyes."

He popped a piece of bubble gum into his mouth. "Mh-hmm."

The jellyfish were a few yards away, looming like purple storm clouds. I took aim with Junior's pistol.

"Threetwo*ONE*," I said, and fired.

The foremost jellyfish erupted into flames. It sagged out of the sky, a sudden sun in the perpetual dusk.

Hollywood ran toward the tarantula. The SCAR's roar cut through the din. Bullets pinged worthlessly off hairy armor. For a moment I saw flames reflected in the huge black eyes. Then the tarantula wheeled and fled.

Behind us, a second jellyfish went up, a dull pop followed by a crackling boom. Then a third, and a fourth. We bolted back the way we'd come. The blaze wouldn't spread far—forest trees were notoriously fire-retardant— but the amount of hydrogen we'd set alight would turn the rest of the vegetation into a whirling inferno.

A safe distance away, we grapple-gunned onto a branch. Fingers of smoke curled after us.

Jittery with adrenaline, I turned on Hollywood.

"You are actually the stupidest person alive," I said.

Hollywood blew a bubble. "Chill."

"You almost got us killed," said Junior, rapping the body camera on Hollywood's chest with gigantic knuckles.

"We were never in any real danger," said Hollywood.

"You're such a fucking idiot," I said.

"Suck a dick."

"Fuck you."

I wanted to rip his throat out. I wanted it so bad for a second that my vision went red and I actually reached toward him, forgetting that we were sixty feet above the forest floor—

Junior smacked my hand down.

"That's enough," he said.

I decided to retie my boots.

"We've still got a few hours until dark," said Junior. "Then two days to get home."

Hollywood blew a bubble, popped it, and slurped it

back in.

"If you do something like that again, I'll kill you," said Junior, grabbing Hollywood's chin and forcing him to make eye contact.

"Real scary," said Hollywood.

I slept much better that second night, and awoke refreshed, emboldened by the adventures of the previous day. This was why I'd left home with everything I owned in a ragged red duffel bag. The miserable months of training had served their purpose. I'd been a loser with no future; now I was a master of nature, a commando, a badass without peer. Yesterday I'd faced the worst the forest could throw at me and survived. Nothing could kill me now.

My feet had barely touched the ground when I heard the screams. Distant but unmistakable: a human female screaming, in agony or fear.

Junior and I froze, but Hollywood didn't waste a second. He clipped the grapple gun to his belt, cradled the SCAR like a football, and crashed off through the undergrowth.

Half a second later, Junior followed. My heart jumped up and down, terror clumping in my throat, but I didn't have a choice. I scrambled after them.

2

If rangers tend to be a little odd, it's because they have a job no truly sane person would want. A ranger's career is extremely lucrative, of course, since the television programs they film pull better ratings than anything except the Super Bowl, but their average lifespan clocks in at a meager four years. Not a lot of time to enjoy the fruits of one's labor. If there's a more dangerous career, we haven't found it yet.

- *Roy LaMonte: Against All Odds*, Theodore Hunker, Salvador Press 2018

The first time I saw Lindsey Li, at six a.m. on the first day of training, she was blocking the entrance to the sleeping quarters, doing pull-ups on the doorframe. She didn't let me through until she'd finished the set.

"You're early," she said when she dropped to the floor. I'd never seen such potent disinterest on someone's face. Later, when I learned the number of other recruits, and the number who would wash out before the final cut, I understood why.

I found my cot and sat down. All five pounds of my worldly possessions had been surrendered at registration, and I felt the missing weight like an amputated limb. I fluffed the flimsy pillow and examined the RangerCorp logo on the sheets. The shoes I'd been issued were too tight.

"Where are you from?" I asked. Li ignored me and went back to pull-ups. I watched the complex movement of muscles in her tank-topped back. Her exhalations were curt and precise. I reclined on my cot and studied the ceiling.

By eight a.m. the room was packed, awash in nervous chatter and the squee of rusty bedsprings. Sergeant Rivers' arrival shut everybody up. He took us outside and set us running. By the end of that first hellish day, he'd ejected thirty recruits. The month of conditioning that followed winnowed us down from two hundred and fifty to seventy-five. I barely survived, but nothing Rivers did could faze Li. Running, climbing, weightlifting, lugging sacks of grain up steep hills . . . she crushed it all.

She'd been training since she was six years old. She was world-class fast, strong, and quick-thinking. I was world-class at nothing. Same with Zip, except when he was on a climbing wall. The two of us outlasted countless stronger, faster, and quicker-thinking recruits because we were simply more stubborn. More desperate. Li continued to ignore us and everyone else until the number of recruits had dwindled to thirty. At that point it was twenty-eight indefatigable freaks of nature, Zip, and me. Then Li started sitting with us in the mess hall.

Up until then she'd invariably sat in the corner by herself. To say that we were unsure how to respond when she plopped down next to Zip would be a stupefying understatement. For a while we kind of just watched her chew. Conversation at the surrounding tables ceased.

"Trade you for your broccoli," she said, offering an apple. Zip wordlessly obliged.

Except for economical movements of her fork, she was motionless. Zip and I exchanged a worried glance and went back to eating.

"I've seen you two up on the roof after curfew," she said after a while.

I blanched. "You're not going to tell anybody, are you?"

"Can I join?"

There was one other thing to mention about Li: it was absolutely impossible to imagine her screaming. She was the type to go teeth-gritting and defiant to the grisliest grave. So even though she was the only woman among the recruits, soon to be the only woman among the active rangers, and therefore the only woman who could conceivably be out here, two days from the coast, where distinctly feminine screams were echoing through the trees—I couldn't quite bring myself to believe that they were coming from her.

3

Date: Wed, 5 April 2017 18:12:04 -0800 (PST)
From: D. Weaver
Subject: subdermals
To: D. Cooper

You've got to talk to Rivers. He gets like this every year. You and I both know there's no room for transparency when it comes to the subdermals. 'Vaccine implants' line has flown for years. It's simple and the recruits accept it without question. Can't change unless we want another PR catastrophe.

Running through the forest is like driving an SUV the wrong way down an interstate: it's possible, technically, but you'd really prefer to avoid getting yourself into that situation to begin with. Every step you take, you have a sneaking suspicion that you missed some deadly clue, that your weight will fall on a mess of leaves concealing a trapdoor spider's lair or a sinkhole hundreds of feet deep. There's no time to check your path, so you pray to God and plant your feet on whatever looks most solid.

I was acutely aware of the danger, and I knew Junior was too, but that didn't stop us from following Hollywood. The screams were getting fewer and further between, but they were still coming.

I burst through a thick patch of razorgrass, covering my face to protect it from lacerations, and stumbled into Junior's back. My momentum carried me past him, and I just had time to realize we were beside an enormous chasm when I tumbled over the edge—

Junior yanked me back with a single huge hand. I'd drawn my pistol as I ran; it slipped out of my grasp and vanished into darkness.

I stood panting beside Junior and Hollywood as we listened for another scream.

"Look," said Junior. On the other side of the chasm stood a tall gray obelisk. It was detailed with a network of fine lines. Against the biological backdrop, its sharp edges were almost profane.

"That's not supposed to be there," said Junior.

Was it throbbing, or was that my imagination? I closed my eyes, rubbed them, and looked again.

"Gimme the floodlight," said Hollywood, peering into the chasm.

Junior rooted mechanically in his pack. Hollywood snatched the floodlight from his hands.

"We should get over there," said Junior. "I've never seen anything like that in the videos, the books, nowhere." He raised a hand above his eyes, squinting. "Are those words?"

Hollywood panned the floodlight over the abyss. The circle of light traveled down the far slope, traversing a network of vines, musty wood, and fungi. It struck me as surreal, almost dreamlike, that he didn't seem to care about the obelisk. I was still shivering from my near-fall. What was he looking for?

Junior yelped. I glanced up just in time to see a shape vanish into the trees.

"There was a person," said Junior, scrambling along the edge. "Tetris, did you see him?"

"Who?"

"I'm going to look," said Junior. "Somebody was over there. I swear to God."

I couldn't detect any movement. For a long, heavy moment, everything was dreadfully still. The only sound was the blood thunking in my temples. Then Hollywood sucked in his breath, the bushes near Junior rustled, and things began to happen very quickly.

Thirty feet below, the floodlight revealed a grinning reptilian face. Clusters of black eyeballs gleamed like river stones. The creature opened its massive jaw, revealing row after row of recurved teeth, and an odor of death wafted up. Out of the gaping mouth came a piercing shriek, the woman's scream we'd heard before, except that this time the noise continued endlessly, increasing in intensity as the creature scrabbled with wicked claws up the wall.

Hollywood dropped the floodlight. It fell toward the monster, the beam of light ricocheting wildly. I turned to shout at Junior, who stared wide-eyed back at us. He could hear the shriek, but hadn't yet glimpsed its source.

"Junior!"

An enormous scorpion, heavy with dull black armor, exploded out of the trees behind him. The stinger snapped, whiplike, and skewered Junior through the torso. The point popped out the front of his chest. As it lifted him off the ground, his feet kicking and his big hands slapping at the segmented tail, Hollywood yanked my arm.

"Run," he said, and led the way.

We barreled back through the razorgrass, stumbled across a tree branch bridging a ravine, and broke into a sprint on the shaking ground beyond.

Behind us, the shriek became a throaty roar, as the reptilian creature sensed the possibility of our escape. I heard a new sound, a heavy whump-whump like mattresses falling to the floor, and snuck a glance back. The creature had taken flight on a set of rippling, scaly wings. It loomed behind and above us, close enough that I could feel its hot breath against my neck.

We weaved between obstacles, Hollywood a few feet ahead of me. No chance of grapple-gunning to safety if the thing could fly. We'd have to lose it in the maze of undergrowth.

We'd just rounded an enormous tree trunk when Hollywood stepped on a moss-and-silk trapdoor and plummeted out of sight. I grabbed the straps of my pack and leapt in after him.

The tunnel was steep and slick, lubricated by webs. There would be a spider in here with us, even now rushing toward this section of its burrow.

I'd dropped my pistol into the chasm. Hollywood might have a chance to produce one of his weapons, but the fall through the trap door would have taken him by surprise, and anyway the spider would get to him in moments.

As my slide accelerated, I saw Hollywood up ahead on a flat spot in the tunnel, headlamp flicked on, hand reaching for the pistol at his side. Beneath him: the spider, hairy legs blurred as it charged from the web-wrapped depths.

One of the spider's front legs pinned Hollywood's gun arm to the floor. The beast leaned in, pedipalps parting to reveal a pair of bulbous fangs—

I fired my grapple gun. The silver spearhead flashed across the cavern, trailing an impossibly thin strand of carbon nanofilament, and shattered the section of carapace beneath the spider's left eye cluster, hardly losing any momentum as it burst out the other side and embedded itself in the wall. Thick green-black goo exploded from the point of impact, showering Hollywood. Countless limbs spasmed in death. With a grunt of exertion, Hollywood planted a foot against the abdomen and shoved, sending the body shuddering back down the tunnel.

"Thanks," he said, wiping the stinking blood out of his eyes.

As I craned my neck to listen out the opening of the burrow, the cries of the winged creature grew fainter. I recalled its scales, a queasy mixture of blue, black and green.

"What was that thing?" I asked.

"That," said Hollywood, "was a fucking dragon."

4

"It's not healthy for our kids to watch this stuff."

"It's just nature."

"I'm sure your viewers agree that it's not just nature."

"Just animals, at the end of the day. And, yes, a few particularly ornery plants."

"Prairie dogs are nature. Lion cubs are nature. This is different."

"They put a parental advisory ahead of every episode. Isn't it your responsibility, as a mother, to keep your children from watching them?"

"You have to draw the line somewhere, Bill. And I'm telling you, these ranger programs are corrupting our youth. My son watched an episode at his friend's house and peed the bed every night for weeks."

"..."

"I don't see what's so funny about that, Bill."

I sat beside Hollywood in a windowless room. Across the table, Sergeant Rivers doodled on a yellow pad. Stars, tornadoes, a skull and crossbones or two. A man in a suit stood behind him, fiddling with his tie.

"Why are we here?" demanded Hollywood. "You've got the bodycam footage."

"Nobody thinks you did anything wrong," said the man behind Rivers in a voice as smooth as Vaseline.

Rivers shifted on his tiny chair. "Agent Cooper just needs you to walk him through it one more time."

There was definitely something going on with Rivers. Frustration? Maybe a sparkle of wry amusement? He'd started drawing a castle. Was working on the parapets.

"We heard screams," I said.

"What kind of screams?" asked Cooper. "It wasn't clear from the bodycam audio."

I shifted. "It sounded like a woman screaming."

Cooper tilted his head like a puzzled dog. "Douglas, what do you think?"

"Nobody calls me that," said Hollywood.

"Did you think the screams sounded human?"

"Yeah, I did," said Hollywood.

"So you chased after them."

Cooper approached the table with lazy steps, hands buried in his pockets. Even sitting down, Rivers was taller.

"Well, excuse me for thinking somebody needed help," said Hollywood.

"Two days into the Pacific Forest? Who could it possibly have been?"

"We thought it might be Li," I said.

"Your fellow recruit, Lindsey Li?"

"Yeah."

The hands emerged from Cooper's pockets and planted themselves on the table.

"You knew her expedition would depart much further down the coast."

"That didn't occur to us at the time, sir."

Cooper's smile reminded me of the dragon's. "Tell me about the clearing. What you found."

"Big pit," said Hollywood.

"Nothing odd?"

Hollywood shrugged.

"Junior saw something," said Cooper.

"There was an obelisk," I said.

"Now we're getting somewhere."

"On the other side of the pit. Junior was going to look."

"Douglas, did you also see the obelisk?"

"Could have been a rock," said Hollywood.

Agent Cooper pulled out a chair beside Rivers and sat, unbuttoning his jacket. Settling back, he steepled his fingers and peered down his slender nose.

"Tell me more about the obelisk," he said after a while.

The image in my head was fuzzy. All I could conjure was the blank look on Junior's face when the scorpion impaled him. As if he expected to wake up from the nightmare at any moment.

"I think there were words on it," I said.

Cooper threw his head back and laughed, startling

Rivers, whose pen snapped. Hollywood nearly knocked me out of my chair trying to dodge the spray of ink.

"Fuck," said Hollywood.

"Watch the language," barked Rivers, holding half a pen in each monstrous paw.

Cooper hadn't taken his eyes off me. "Are you a conspiracy theorist?"

"No, sir."

"Hieroglyphic script on mysterious monuments... sounds like the kind of ridiculous fantasy those people trot out to justify their hypotheses about an ancient civilization hidden beneath the trees."

"I'm not familiar, sir."

"I think I agree with Douglas. It was probably just a rock."

"If you say so, sir."

Cooper leaned close. I examined the doughy folds of his face, his beady little pupils.

"Can I trust you not to spread this 'obelisk' story? The nutjobs have enough to work with already. The last thing we need is any more misinformation."

Hollywood snorted. "Is that what this is about?"

"Of course not," said Cooper. "This is about the young man, Junior, and the unfortunate circumstances surrounding his death. Can you talk me through the events from your perspective?"

It was a long, silent drive back to training camp. Riding with Rivers was always an ordeal, since his single eye and generally forceful disposition tended to send him careening into lanes already occupied by unsuspecting motorists. He never checked his blind spots, just wrenched the wheel and trusted everyone else to get out of the way.

That night I couldn't fall asleep, so I tiptoed outside. It was chilly. Clouds of insects swarmed the lights that lined the path to the grapple gun course. I went to the corner of the barracks and climbed the gutter.

Li was already up there, sitting on the edge of the roof.

"Hi," I said. She didn't respond. I sat beside her. She squinted at something in the darkness across the training field.

"Hollywood said you thought you heard me screaming," she said.

"Maybe."

She shook her head. "Why?"

"It sounded like a girl."

"Fuck off."

"What?"

She winged a shard of brick at a light post below. The bulb shattered.

"If I'd been there, Junior wouldn't have died," she said.

I pinched the loose skin on my kneecaps and twisted, hard.

"My dad told me that some things mimic human noises. Screams, shouts, laughter," she said.

"Never came up in class."

"Pretty rare, I think. But I would have known."

"I didn't want to go. Hollywood went, we followed."

"You could have stopped him."

"Maybe."

We sat in silence. I went over the scene in my head: Hollywood breaking into a sprint, the slow seconds before he slipped out of sight. Could I have convinced him to come back?

"How do you think they learn those noises?"

"Hmm?" I said.

"The human noises. How do they learn those screams? You think rangers teach them, when they die?"

"Could be."

"Doesn't explain the laughter, though."

I shivered. "Cold out here."

"It doesn't add up, Tetris. That everything in the forest is just a dumb animal. I don't buy it."

I considered telling her about the obelisk. About the person Junior thought he saw. After the talk with Agent Cooper, though, I kept my mouth shut. She wouldn't believe me anyway.

"Our first couple of weeks," she said, "Junior was the only one who treated me like a normal person."

It was too dark to see her face.

"What about me?"

"Oh, come on."

We watched moths spar with the remaining lamps.

"I want to get some sleep," she said. "No way Rivers will give us a break tomorrow just because Junior's gone."

When she reached the edge of the roof, she paused. Scratched the back of her head and cleared her throat.

"Don't beat yourself up, Tetris," she said. "It wasn't your fault."

After a long and awkward moment, she climbed down the gutter. I stayed up there for a long time, looking at the stars.

"Sorry, Junior," I said, but my voice sounded flat and cold.

5

Air Force fighter jets brought down a 1,200-ton tentacled creature on Monday after it penetrated the Coast Guard perimeter west of Los Angeles. 50 were killed and at least 300 injured in the rampage, the worst since 2004. In Washington, questions have once again been raised as to the efficacy of current Coast Guard countermeasures.

"Bigger guns would certainly go a long way," Coast Guard chief Donald McCarthy told the Post.

A few years later, Zip and I drove down to Portland to meet Li's family. We took Zip's pride and joy, a decades-old, beat-up red Corvette. The roof was cracked, so it leaked when it rained, which in Seattle was a fairly significant issue, and the seat belts didn't work—they just hung across your chest like lasagna noodles—but Zip's love for the car was boundless and all-forgiving.

"I don't understand your refusal to buy a new car," I said, gripping the edge of my seat as the scarlet death trap rattled over a pothole. "What else are you doing with those paychecks?"

"Saving," said Zip. "I'm not—"

"—a big spender, yeah."

I fingered my two thousand-dollar watch. In two years as a ranger I'd acquired a spacious apartment and an orange muscle car, taken trips to Europe and Asia, and outfitted myself with a wardrobe that was, if not fashionable, then at least expensive. Meanwhile my bank account hovered around empty, and my credit card bills were multiplying.

Zip patted the dashboard. "I'm going to drive this thing until the wheels fall off, and then I'm going to buy new wheels."

I'd taken a rough fall at the bouldering gym the day before, and my ankle was killing me. Climbing with Zip was humbling. Not as bad as when we'd first started, when I'd lacked the technique to tackle anything higher than a V3, but still pretty bad. Zip annihilated routes with holds the depth of credit cards, moving like a praying mantis, relentless and self-assured. Even after all the practice, I still found myself trembling through routes a person with half my strength and a bit more technique could have managed with ease.

You could tell Zip was good by the way veteran climbers watched him. Respect and jealousy battled it out on their leathery faces. Sometimes people clapped.

The Li family lived in a brick mansion up on a hill. Li's silver convertible was in the driveway. When we rang the doorbell I considered running. What if they laid out a bunch of little forks and spoons, and I didn't know which to use for what?

Zip was as calm as ever, though his right hand curled and uncurled, squeezing an imaginary tennis ball. His family had been just as dysfunctional as mine. Neither of us would ever have invited our friends over.

I fidgeted with my tie. Today was the first time I'd seen Zip in a button-up. It was a size too small. I hadn't noticed until it was far too late.

The door opened.

We were not devoured.

It was pretty awkward, though. I went for the handshake while Mr. Li offered a hug; I switched mid-flight to go for the hug and ate a massive shoulder as he tried to match a shake no longer being offered... Zip barged through the door after me, discovered that there wasn't enough room in the foyer for all five of us, and tried to step back outside just as Mrs. Li offered her own hug. Zip whipped back around to return the hug, which she'd already abandoned, then tried to pretend that he hadn't seen it, fake-stumbling to explain all the jerky movements, except that he ended up actual-stumbling and knocked an expensive-looking urn off its table. Li caught it, of course.

"So," said Mr. Li, beaming at his daughter over the dinner table, "You've been on how many expeditions together, now, the three of you? Nine?"

"Thought it was ten," said Zip.

I lifted mashed potatoes to my mouth. Noticing Mr. Li looking my way, I nodded, hastening to swallow.

"We're shooting for the record," I said.

"Which one?"

"Most expeditions by the same trio," said Li. "Record is twenty-six."

"Sixteen more expeditions?" exclaimed Mrs. Li.

"Jeez, Mom, have a little faith."

Mrs. Li sawed her steak vigorously. I gathered there was something of an ideological divide in the Li household when it came to Li's career choice.

"You don't have to worry, Mrs. Li," said Zip, puffing out his chest as his shirt buttons held on for dear life. "She's in strong, capable, dare I say *dashing* hands."

"Ha," barked Li. "When that velociraptor went for your esophagus, who, exactly, evaporated its face?"

"What about when you were about to step on that boomslug?" said Zip. "Who was it, again, who said 'Li, please take care not to step on that boomslug, lest you perish in an immolation of your own creation?'"

"I wasn't about to step on anything," said Li. "I was well aware of the slug, and as I recall, your oafish shout in that instance caused quite the—"

"Li thinks she's our daddy."

"You're damn right I'm your daddy."

"Boomslug?" said Mrs. Li weakly.

Zip crunched into a Brussels sprout. "Explosive invertebrate, bright orange, very bad to step on, but luckily pretty hard to miss, unless you're—"

"—which is why I didn't miss it, dumbass, I—"

"I saved Li from a crab once," I said.

"Zip would have fallen in those beetleflowers if I hadn't—"

"Anyway I'm like eighty-five percent sure I had the velociraptor situation under control."

"That is such a load of—"

Mr. Li cleared his throat. Silence materialized.

"As long as we're trading stories," he said, "has she told you the one about the lions?"

"Dad."

"It's a great story."

"It really isn't."

"Go on," said Zip.

Li glowered at him. Zip stuck out his tongue.

"It happened on a trip to the zoo," said Mr. Li, "when Lindsey was seven years old."

Mrs. Li laid a hand on his arm. "This still gives me nightmares."

"We stopped to consult a map, and when we looked up, she was gone."

"Poof."

"We searched the area—no luck. It was summer, and the crowds were positively teeming. Eventually we decided to find an information booth, a security guard, somebody who could help. Except there were no employees in sight. One finally went tearing by, holding his hat to his head. I grabbed his arm. What was going on?"

"Some kid had gotten into the lion enclosure," said Mrs. Li.

Zip whooped.

"We found her cuddling with a lioness," said Mr. Li. "They hadn't laid a paw on her."

"It was all over the news," said Mrs. Li.

"She was famous."

"Twelve million views."

"An appearance on a late-night television program."

Mrs. Li wiped her lips. "I still think that's why she became a ranger."

"Not true," said Li.

"The things you put me through," said Mrs. Li, turning to me. "What about your parents? Don't they worry?"

The last time I'd heard from my dad was the day I left home, when he'd unleashed one last eyeball-bulging rant. Did that count? I looked to Zip for help.

"My parents are too busy working to worry," he said.

Mrs. Li narrowed her eyes, and Zip looked sheepish for perhaps the first time ever, but then Mr. Li boomed a laugh.

"Understandable," he said, putting a hand on his wife's shoulder. "Lucy's a neurosurgeon, so God knows she works hard. Me, on the other hand..."

"You have your gardening," said Mrs. Li.

Now Mr. Li joined Zip in looking sheepish.

"Have to keep busy somehow," he said.

This was a man who had battled the forest for nearly a decade. Thirty years older than Zip or me, he maintained comparable muscle mass. It was simply impossible to imagine his hands cupping a plant bulb or trimming a rose bush. Tearing weeds out of the ground, though: that I could imagine him doing. Mercilessly.

"This expedition record," said Mrs. Li, "who holds it currently?

"Roy LaMonte and the Briggs brothers," said Li.

"I knew Roy," said Mr. Li. "Fantastic poker player. Terrific mustache. Shame the way things turned out."

"Still better than what happened to the Briggs brothers," said Li. She stabbed with relish at her Brussels sprouts. "Mom, how come you never made these when I was growing up?"

"Your father does all the cooking these days, dear," said Mrs. Li. "Mind if I ask what happened to the Briggs brothers?"

Mr. Li clicked his tongue. "Not appropriate dinner conversation, I'm afraid. Suffice it to say that the forest got them."

"Pass the salt, please," said Li.

"The steak's more than salty enough as it is," said Mrs. Li. "You'll give yourself a heart attack."

Li's incisors gleamed. "Least of my worries, Ma."

Mrs. Li passed the salt.

"Poor Roy," mused Mr. Li. "After that trip—amazing that he made it out, by the way—he was raving mad. Wouldn't stop talking about the things he'd supposedly seen."

"What'd he think he saw?" I asked.

"Fantasies. Towers, pyramids, you get the idea. People, too."

My fork, laden with another mound of potatoes, froze just short of my mouth.

Mr. Li raised a silver-flecked eyebrow. "Is something wrong?"

The look Li gave me said: Tell me later.

"No," I said, and cleared my throat.

That night, Zip and I flipped a coin to see who got the guest bed. I lost and headed to the living room to set up on the couch.

I was digging for my toothbrush when Li came down the stairs. She looked amazing. I couldn't quite figure out why—the pajamas weren't revealing or form-fitting, so maybe it was the shapelessness itself that made it hot, somehow—but for a couple moments I forgot not only what she'd come down to talk about, but also the English language and my own name besides.

"What was that?" she asked.

"Uhm?"

"You know what I'm talking about."

I gave up on the toothbrush and sat back on the couch. "It's probably nothing."

Li perched, cross-legged, on an armchair across from

me. "Tell me, Tetris."

I took off my watch and stared at it. The ticks reverberated in my fingertips.

"Before Junior died," I said, "I thought I saw something. Something like what your dad described, across the chasm."

Shadows cast Li's features into stark angles and planes.

"An obelisk," I said. "Script all over it. Junior saw it too. That's why he left us behind."

"And you thought Roy LaMonte—"

"Junior said he saw a person."

"Like, a human person?"

"That's all he said. I didn't see anything. Well, I saw something, but I couldn't tell what it was."

I strained to picture the scene, the shape vanishing into the forest. Might as well have tried to remember my mother's face.

Li stared out the window. I looked too. There was nothing to see. I imagined Junior stepping into view, pressing his face against the glass. In my imagination, his eyes were shiny and black, even the parts that should have been white. When he opened his mouth, blood dribbled over his parched bottom lip.

My eyes watered. I peeled my gaze away from the window.

"You sure you saw something man-made?" said Li.

"I don't know," I said.

"I wonder," said Li, unfolding her legs.

"What?"

"Nothing."

She stretched, hands linked above her head. At the apex of the stretch, her shirt lifted up just far enough to reveal a strip of midriff. I averted my eyes.

"Enjoy the couch," she said.

"Beats a tree branch."

I watched her climb the stairs.

When she was gone, I went to the bathroom and brushed my teeth. Then I returned to the living room and turned off the lights. The whole time, I studiously avoided glancing out any of the windows.

Immediately after falling asleep, I began to dream. I stood by the chasm in the forest where Junior had died. No matter how I stared into the darkness, though, I couldn't make out the obelisk on the other side.

The chasm seemed much deeper and darker than before. I knew that if I stood beside it too much longer, it would drag me in, but my feet stayed rooted to the ground.

At first, the forest was silent, but after a while I began to hear a rustling.

When I turned around, Junior was there, held aloft by the scorpion that had killed him. The stinger poked out through his chest, but his legs were still, not kicking the way I remembered. The scorpion blinked its many eyes, and I got the feeling it wanted to say something, if only its mouthparts were capable of articulating more than a complicated hiss.

"TETRIS," said Junior, in a voice far too deep, as blood dribbled down his chin.

Reluctantly, I brought my gaze up to his face. His eyes were as black and shiny as the scorpion's.

"I'm sorry, Junior," I said.

"Under your skin," said Junior in that awful, grating voice. His mouth was full of worms. "Your skin, Tetris. You have to know—"

I jolted awake before I could hear any more. Sweat slicked my body from neck to ankles, and my heart thumped violently against my ribs.

6

We've figured out physics. We've put humans in orbit, on the moon, and in a few years we'll be sending them to Mars. We've mapped the globe, split the atom, cured cancer, and perfected plumbing. But there's still one question we haven't answered. One place right here on Earth that remains a total mystery, because we've only scratched its surface: the World Forest. That's what rangers are for.

- RangerCorp promotional brochure

On the ninth day of our eleventh expedition, with a lemony aroma in the air, we came across a creeper vine.

"Check it out," said Li, slinging the SCAR-17 across her back.

I crouched beside her. The vine was thick and sinewy, an inert green snake. It trailed into a crevice a few feet away.

Li gave it a poke with a stick. The vine tugged the stick from her hand and hissed out of sight.

A year or two earlier, this would have filled me with dread. Now I just grinned, imagining the plant's frustration when it discovered that its tendril had been fooled. No tasty morsel this time.

This expedition, we'd set out much further down the coast, near San Diego. The previous team assigned to this region had gone missing, presumed dead. Apart from a slight temperature increase, it was more or less the same forest.

"I was thinking about what you said, Tetris," said Zip.

"Hmm?"

"About me not spending my money."

"Oh."

"There's one thing I'd blow it on."

"Girls."

"Well, I mean, other than that."

"Climbing gear."

"Got plenty of that already."

"As far as I know, those are the only expensive things you like. So."

"Tacos."

"Tacos. Are not expensive."

"I mean the best tacos. In the world."

"Even good tacos are not expensive."

"Somewhere out there, there is a man who has spent his entire life making tacos."

"Or woman," said Li.

"And this man—"

"Or woman."

"—who I presume lives on a Mexican mountaintop somewhere, far from distractions, and makes tacos day in and day out, feeding them to the wildlife, because the customer is a hassle, see, the tacos themselves are the point—"

I had a bug bite the diameter of a quarter on my neck, but I refused to scratch it.

"Impoverished taco hermit is about the worst job I can think of," I said.

"You clearly haven't worked in a funeral home," said Zip.

"Please, God, no, I take it back."

"When I was fifteen, I started helping my dad with the embalming."

"Here we go."

"You don't want to know what we had to do to those bodies," said Zip.

"No more than the first time."

"First you suck out all the blood and replace it with embalming fluid. Fasten the eyes and mouth shut. All the leak-prone orifices have to be plugged. If a person's been decapitated or something, you have to piece them back together."

"No doubt. No doubt."

"A lot of the time when we pump the embalming fluid in, the deceased gets an erection. If it's a dude. We have to, like, tape it to his leg."

This was new information. The image rose at once: a mourning family crowded around an open casket, everyone studiously ignoring the tent in the pants of the silver-haired occupant.

"The worst I saw was a guy who got run over by a forklift."

"Totally 'forked' up, huh?"

"Tore his legs off. Dragged his top half across ten yards of gravel."

"Real talk: how does that even happen?"

"Dunno. Runaway forklift."

"Those can't possibly go more than ten, fifteen miles an hour."

"My dad was an artist. Sewed the two halves together, repaired the skin, and rebuilt the skull with putty. You would have thought he died of a heart attack."

I thought of my brother, small and bald and cold in the casket.

"People say the forest's so dangerous," said Zip, "but out on land you can get torn to shreds by a forklift. You can slip off a grapple gun course. You can trip getting off the bus and break your neck."

"Wow, you might be on to something," I said. "Wait— which is the place with snakes the size of subway trains, again?"

"Dead is dead," said Zip. "It doesn't matter whether it was a drunk driver or a subway snake that killed you."

We edged around a ravine as a distant creature skreeled and sang.

"What you really have to watch out for," said Li, "is an inebriated subway snake."

Zip had just opened his mouth to respond when a clatter of chitinous legs rose from below. We drew our grapple guns and rocketed away.

A flood of giant spiders burst through the floor, scrabbling over each other and onto the trunk of our tree. Up they climbed, zeroing in like bloodhounds drawn to a scent.

"There," said Li, pointing at a tree some distance away. We fired our grapple guns and swung across. The rush of air made my eyes water. Spiders flooded after us. Tens of thousands of them. I'd never seen anything like it. The producers would eat this footage up if we survived long enough to bring it home.

By the time we'd landed and rearmed our grapple guns, the spiders were halfway up this tree too.

"We've gotta go higher," said Zip.

Only sunlight could drive these things away. It was worth the risk of brushing the canopy. Our grapple guns fired, one after the other, and we zipped to a thick branch far above. The spiders kept coming.

"If y'all have any bright ideas, I'm listening," said Li.

At this altitude, the tree's sway was noticeable. Another jump and we'd be in the canopy proper, where the grapple guns were useless.

"They'll stop climbing," said Zip.

The spiders continued climbing.

"You'd think the light would have turned them away by

now," said Li.

There was something large and scaly hidden in the leaves twenty or thirty feet above us. Four orange eyes blinked in counter-clockwise order, then vanished.

The spiders knocked each other off as they flowed up the trunk, hundreds flailing through empty air at any given time, crunching into the horde like leggy cannonballs.

"Another tree," I said. "They'll have to climb the whole thing again."

We swung to another tree. Sure enough, the flood of spiders began scaling this one too. From this height, their shapes were indistinguishable. They were an amorphous black mass, geologic in scale.

The ones on our previous tree continued to climb. It was clear that they intended to skitter across and sandwich us from above.

"We can hardly be worth the effort they're exerting," I said.

"Speak for yourself," said Zip.

"They'll give up," said Li, pointing out another tree.

But spiders were already scaling that one, along with every other tree in the vicinity. The net had begun to close.

An ominous rumble joined the maelstrom. As our tree shuddered, the spider-covered ground puckered and swelled. Out burst the twirling maw of a creature so immense it could have swallowed the Washington Monument. All mouth and neck, with no eyes I could see, the worm didn't eat the spiders so much as drink them, sucking them down its bright pink throat.

Our tree teetered, its root network upended.

"Go," shouted Li, and we fired our grapple guns, swinging free just as the tree went thundering down. The impact sent others tumbling like gigantic, groaning dominoes. Denizens of the canopy shrieked and roared, searching for a stable place to take hold. A dragonfly zipped by in a panic, and enormous mosquitoes cruised aimlessly overhead.

We prepared our grapple guns again. The spiders had become the prey. Away they scuttled, retreating into to the tangled depths as the pink creature slurped them down like water droplets off a leaf.

A few jumps later, when we paused to catch our breath, I began to shudder. I clamped my mouth shut, but my chest shook harder and harder, until finally it all came spilling out, a deluge of painful, hiccuping laughter. Zip and Li must have felt it too, because they grinned like toddlers meeting a cat for the first time.

"Those stupid fucking spiders," I choked, wiping my eyes on my sleeve. "Did you see—did you see?"

Li spat. The three of us watched the glob of spittle tumble, shrink, and vanish.

"Fuck," she said, savoring the word, drawing it out like a death row inmate taking her last drag of a cigarette. "I love you guys."

Zip snickered.

"Yeah, okay, I take that back," she said.

Warmth pulsated in my veins. This was why I was here.

Zip unwrapped a protein bar and took a bite.

"I've got a story," he said with his mouth full.

"Always bragging about your conquests," said Li.

"Not that kind of story," said Zip.

I grabbed a protein bar of my own.

"Sunday afternoon," said Zip, "I roll out of bed, put on my flip-flops, and head to the gas station for a bite to eat."

"You're the only person making three hundred grand a year who's ever used 'gas station' and 'bite to eat' in the same sentence," said Li.

"I grab the usual—hot dog, sour gummy worms, onion rings, 76-oz blue slushie—and I've got all this shit cradled in my arms as I go flip-flopping up to the register."

Zip took a big gulp from his canteen.

"So I'm standing there with my arms full, trying to figure out how to retrieve my wallet from my pajama pants, and the cashier is glaring at me, because no matter how many days in a row he sees me, I am still a buff black man, and therefore probably a criminal. Same old everyday shit."

"Downright quotidian," said Li.

"Until a skinhead walks in and pulls a gun. Shirtless, full-body tattoo, swastikas aplenty, red eyes, the classic package. Standard citizen, at this point, would be unnerved. But I'm three feet from this thug as he waves the pistol, bellowing about the Reichstag or whatever, and all I can do is stare at his twiggy little legs. Up top he's got biceps, shoulders, et cetera. Except he's never heard of squats, never caught wind of dead lifts, and he looks like you could knock him over with a squirt gun.

"Well, I must have chuckled, because this fine Southern gentleman invades my personal space, leans over me, and positively shrieks the N-word.

"'*Gib mir dein wallet*,' he screams, and jams the pistol in my sternum, which knocks the slushie out of my arms. This makes me very upset. It is his first major error.

"I tell him no problem, one wallet coming right up. I lean down and place the hot dog, onion rings, and gummy worms beside the spreading slushie mountain. Then I straighten, produce my wallet, and hand it to him. The whole time, we're staring right in each other's eyes, it's like the climax of a fucking rom-com.

"He's got my wallet now, and this is where he makes his second mistake, because he pulls that Glock back and flips the wallet with his other hand to see what's in there. Soon as he breaks eye contact I leap to the side and grab his arm—the gun goes off, BLAM! Shatters the glass in the beer section—and I snap his wrist. Gun falls into the slushie puddle, I kick it away, and as this dude's starting to scream I shove his legs out from under him and slam his face on the linoleum. And I swear to you, friends—I swear that this man's bald head bounced."

"Every word of that story is imaginary," said Li.

"I have the police report to prove it," said Zip. "Remind me to show you when we get back."

"What happened next?" I asked.

"Thug was out cold in a puddle of blue-raspberry blood. Cashier issued another slushie free of charge, so I sipped on that until the police arrived."

"You crack his skull open?" I asked, hungry for details. What had the impact sounded like? Had his body spasmed around, or gone straight limp?

Zip shrugged. "I didn't hang around long. Had a date that afternoon."

"Oh, of course," said Li.

"Point is," said Zip, "I think this job changes us. Even with that gun against my chest, I wasn't scared."

"I bet that asshole's skull cracked wide open," I said, satisfied by the thought. "I bet he's fucking dead."

"Huh," said Zip, and took another drink from his canteen.

7

On the eleventh morning of our expedition, we came to the edge of a canyon.

It was a gash so broad and deep that the canopy could scarcely bandage it. Branches strained to nuzzle across the gap. Sunlight snuck through, harsher than a camera flash, and painted jittery shadows against the chasm's walls.

The light pierced a mile into the depths, a descent criss-crossed by fat, grasping roots. Nothing moved.

We set out along the edge. Half an hour later, we found a fallen tree that bridged the gap. The ravine curved away forever. I probed a sore tooth with my tongue. The bridge-tree must have fallen recently, because blue sky poured through a canopy-wound overhead.

Blue was a rarity in the forest, existing only to denote poison. For instance: blue frogs the size of meat lockers.

They would leave you alone, but if you ever had the misfortune to touch one, the toxins coating their skin would squirm through your pores and liquefy your organs.

We crossed, quickly but carefully, along the very center of the trunk. Safe among the trees on the other side, I exhaled.

"Felt like an ant on the sidewalk out there," I said.

Zip adjusted the straps of his pack. "Twelve-year-old me must have murdered twelve billion of those."

"How unique," said Li.

"I don't think you grasp how seriously I took my quest of entomologiful eradication."

"Entomological."

"'Fuck ants,' essentially," said Zip. He tried to turn a shudder into a shrug. "I hate ants."

That night, a storm rolled over the forest. As we settled into our sleeping bags, a soothing drone of raindrops masked the normal nighttime sounds. Distant thunder grumbled. Rainwater slithered through the leaves and fell in intermittent three-hundred-foot pillars.

The way our tree swayed back and forth, you could tell that the storm was stirring up fierce winds above the canopy, but by the time it reached us, the gale was toothless. A gentle swirl of fresh, wet air was all that remained, and we drank it in with relish.

Kept awake by the sound of rain, I stared out the top of my sleeping bag and remembered Boy Scouts. On a camping trip at Badger Falls, when I was thirteen, it had rained every night for a week. On that trip, I'd been the only kid without a dad. At night I pressed the wall of the tent and watched the droplets accumulate. Hoping to taste pure rainwater, I licked up some moisture I collected this way, but it tasted like my palm—the acrylic sting of bug spray mixed with salty sweat.

In the forest, rangers collected water via condensation nets. Tonight, with the rainfall providing extra moisture, those nets would fill our canteens in minutes. That was pure rainwater, or close enough, but by the time you took a drink, it tasted like the canteen.

Asleep at last, I stood on the forest floor, in the dark, alone. The storm had passed, and all was still, until a thousand spiders crawled up from below. They encircled me, crowding against each other so that their hairy legs scrabbled and interlocked. Fangs gleamed between innumerable pedipalps, but the fear I felt seemed disconnected from the spiders somehow.

Out of the darkness swayed Junior, held aloft by the scorpion's stinger.

"Tetris," he said with a carnivorous smile. His teeth were much too long.

I peered into his black eyes.

"You haven't been listening to me," said Junior, his voice resonating in my bones.

The spiders chittered and rubbed their mandibles together. They coated the tree trunks, clinging to the bark with hooked feet, a swarm ten thousand strong, every eye fixed on me.

"It's under your skin, Tetris."

I could feel it, the skin of my neck crawling, something wriggling to escape. I fought the urge to tear myself open. My palms stung, and I discovered that my fists were clenched, the fingernails digging deep ruts. Any moment now, the nails would burst out the backs of my hands...

"Can't you leave me alone?" I begged.

The forest was silent. Junior considered my words. The spiders shifted their focus to him, waiting for the response.

"No," said Junior at last, and the horde of spiders writhed, screaming.

The scorpion clacked its claws, and silence fell again, although the spiders continued to spasm. Their mouthparts flagellated madly.

"Trust your eyes, Tetris," said Junior, oblivious to the roiling chaos. "Trust nothing else."

The floor gave way, and I fell into bottomless darkness, unspeakable shapes contorting and shrieking all around me.

In the morning I had purple crescents underneath my eyes.

"What kept you up?" asked Li.

Zip, packing his sleeping bag, thought the question was meant for him.

"I slept like a koala," he said. "Love it when it rains."

"Not you. Tetris looks like a gorilla punched him in each eye."

"I punched him back," I said.

"I'm sure you did."

"You think there's a way they could make these breakfast bars taste better, but they don't bother, because it's cheaper this way?" asked Zip, unwrapping one as he spoke.

"Is that mulch or plastic?" I asked, grabbing one out of my own pack.

"Mulch," said Zip.

"Trade you," I suggested. Plastic, which was supposed to taste like key lime pie, left a slick, acrid residue on the roof of your mouth. The blueberry bars might taste like mulch, but at least they went down properly.

Zip shrugged and tossed it over. When I tossed mine, I must have put some crazy spin on it, because it bounced off Zip's hand and tumbled out of the tree.

"God damn it, Tetris," said Zip, peering after it. "I'm never gonna find that thing."

We finished packing and rappelled down. As Li checked the magazine in the SCAR, Zip rooted through the brush for his breakfast.

I scanned the undergrowth, half-expecting to see dream-Junior's smirking face. My jaw throbbed. I placed fingers against the base of my ear and felt the joint pop. Must have been gritting my teeth again. Wearing my molars down to nubs.

Zip's yelp shattered the silence. Something that sounded like a bird, but was almost certainly not a bird, squawked three times in response.

"Are you nuts?" hissed Li.

"Look at this," said Zip.

"Keep it down," said Li, but she went to look. I stayed where I was.

Newly-fallen leaves covered the ground. They'd shrivel and lose their color within a few hours, but for now they draped like veiny doormats all around. Not for the first time, I marveled at their size. Skeletons of tough cellulose kept the green skin rigid, like bones in a bat wing.

Actually, it was kites they reminded me of. I wondered if you could get a forest leaf to fly, at least in the brief period before it began to decay. Not that I'd ever—

"Tetris, you've gotta see this," said Li.

"What's that look like to you?" asked Zip.

A prickling chill started at my scalp and broadened as it went. Past the tangled matrix of branches and leaves was a gray tablet etched with complicated symbols.

"Is that what you told me about?" asked Li, hunched over my shoulder.

"You guys keeping secrets from me?" said Zip, letting the bush wobble back into place.

"I think it is," I said, scratching my neck.

Li stowed the rifle and wrenched away chunks of vegetation. Zip and I bent to help. Much of the tablet lay underground, so we dug with our fingers. Soon the soil was everywhere: caked under our nails, smeared on our cheeks, gritting between our teeth.

I couldn't believe it. Right there, a few inches away, was a tangible contradiction of everything we'd been taught about the world. Perhaps it was a sci-fi movie prop that had dropped out of a plane? The symbols resembled no language I'd ever seen. They were all sharp corners and fine details. Hieroglyphs? No two were alike. The symbols were large, several inches across, and their contours were complicated by fractal appendages.

When I'd seen the obelisk, it had been too far away to judge its composition. With my hands against the gray tablet, I was even more confused. The material was too uniform, too featureless, to be stone. Yet it was cool and smooth as a granite countertop.

Not metal. Not plastic. But not stone, either, at least no stone I'd ever seen.

"You guys have got to tell me what this is," said Zip.

"I've got no fucking clue," said Li. "Tetris told me he saw something covered in symbols. That's the extent of my expertise, here."

I sat back on my heels. "This is a lot smaller, but yeah, it looks similar."

"There's no way," said Zip, scanning the treeline.

The cuts in my palms sang.

"I'm freaking out, guys," said Zip.

"Cool it," said Li. "We'll take pictures and bail. Once we're out, somebody will tell us what we're looking at."

I remembered Agent Cooper leaning over the table, breathing his acrid mouthwash breath.

"They know," I said.

"What?"

"I think they know," I said. "Those fuckers. I think they know."

"Stay with me, Tetris," said Zip.

"When Junior died, the FBI questioned me and Hollywood," I said. "I thought they wanted to know what happened with Junior, but the government guy, the agent, he didn't care about that. What he cared about was the obelisk."

"Obelisk, right." Zip glanced at Li. "Obelisk?"

"It's why Junior died," I said, suddenly exhausted. "He was going to look. They must have seen it in our footage, flagged it down."

Zip nodded several times. "Yes yes yes. Okay. Yes. Alright. Just so you know, though, you sound like an absolute wacko."

"That's what the agent said!"

"Mhhmm."

"Remember the story Li's dad told? Roy LaMonte saw obelisks, structures, people—"

"LaMonte was a nutjob," said Zip. "That guy could find evidence of ancient civilizations in a Burger Hut parking lot."

Li's fingertips tapped the SCAR's stock.

"Oh, come on," said Zip, "you can't possibly believe this."

"The Briggs brothers died on that trip," she said.

"Wouldn't he have shown the pictures? Taken a video?"

"It all goes through the government first," I said. "It's a condition of the subsidies. They could have censored it."

We stared at the tablet. Was that a slight glow,

hovering around the edges, or was it my imagination?

"You realize that the FBI will see our footage, too," said Zip. "The body cameras. Everything we're saying right now is recorded. If you're right, and they're trying to cover something up, we are totally fucked. As soon as we turn this in, they'll lock us away, or worse."

"So we don't turn it in," said Li. "We take the footage straight to the news networks."

I considered that. It wasn't like they were waiting for us when we came out of the forest. Our return wasn't a scheduled event. Typically, we headed as close to east as we could manage, and wherever we wound up on the coastline, we radioed for pick-up. We could slide under the radar and hitchhike to the nearest town. At any public library, we could hop on computers, make copies of the evidence, and send it everywhere, like an email chain letter. Backups upon backups.

"I'm with you," I said.

Zip ran a finger along an indented symbol. His shoulders shrank. For a moment he resembled a middle-schooler, disappointed in his report card, imagining the look on his father's face when he brought it home.

"I wish we'd never found this," he said.

"Me too," I said, startled to discover that it was a lie.

8

We couldn't pull ourselves away.

"What if there's a whole city up ahead?" said Li.

I wiped my palms on my pants to sop up the sweat, but the fabric only drew further moisture from my pores.

"This is making my nuts shrivel up," said Zip. "I've got a couple of raisins down there."

I kept expecting the tablet to vanish the second I dragged my eyes away.

"We should turn around," said Li, but she didn't move. The toe of her boot drew circles in the dirt.

"Yes, heading for shore is definitively correct," said Zip, who also didn't move.

Strains of a violent argument reached our ears. Deep bellows, like an elephant defending its water hole, followed by a rapid-fire series of avian shrieks.

"Fuck it," I said, checking the mag in my pistol. "Let's go."

Onward we went, miners drawn into unplumbed depths by visions of sparkling jewels. We didn't find a city. For five hours, we didn't find anything at all, except endless, identical trees. Tangled vines and towers of steaming excrement began to seem familiar, as if we were walking in circles, although I'd been checking my compass every five minutes. Our voices grew taut and thin. Zip spat strands of phlegm into the undergrowth, and I wondered if his mouth had the same sulfurous taste that mine did.

Eventually we stopped for lunch.

"I wonder if Sergeant Rivers knew about this," said Li around a mouthful of protein bar.

I thought back to the interrogation, the look on Rivers' face.

"No clue," I said.

Zip balled up a wrapper and hurled it into a ravine.

Li scratched her nose with the back of her arm. "You guys hear how he lost his eye?"

"I suppose you're going to tell us," said Zip.

"One of his teammates got nabbed by a creeper vine."

I leaned against a tree trunk and counted blades of razorgrass. Heavy perfume wafted from some flowerbank out of sight. I'd already heard the story, but I didn't mind listening to Li's voice.

"Per company policy, Rivers and his remaining partner were supposed to turn around. Instead they rappelled down the hole."

"Dun dun dunnn," said Zip.

"There was a cavern underneath. No bottom in sight. The plant was perched on a fallen tree with vines coming off it like puppet strings. Rivers got down there and pulled the missing guy out, but it had already started to digest him."

Zip probed his ear with a pinky finger. "And then he got acid in his eye. The end."

"Even less cool than that. On the way up, something huge grabbed his partner, who was carrying the unconscious guy. Rivers kept going, but the grapple line came whipping down and pow—no more eye."

"There's a moral in there somewhere," said Zip, scrunching his face in mock concentration.

After lunch we went back to walking. Just when I'd begun to think that there was nothing out here, we found a tall gray pillar in a clearing no different from the thousands of others we'd crossed.

It was the biggest structure so far. Featureless and smooth, it was bare of hieroglyphs except for a convoluted labyrinth etched at its peak. On the far side of the clearing, a trio of enormous ants wriggled in the tangled threads of a seventeen-story spider web.

Li crept closer to the gray structure, and I followed, keeping an eye on the wobbling web.

"I don't like this," said Zip.

I laid both palms against the obelisk. It was cool and damp as a stone plucked from a riverbed, with the same smell of earthy nothingness.

"Guys, come on," said Zip, as a pair of bloated red spiders crept out of the canopy. Their titanic abdomens throbbed like human hearts.

"Gimme a lift, Tetris," said Li, peering at the markings. I bent, allowing her to clamber onto my shoulders.

The spiders ambled down the web. Their lazy movements suggested that they'd already feasted today, and the ants were a happy surprise, like a slice of cake discovered in the fridge. The larger spider grasped an ant and administered a bite. At first the gyrations only intensified, but after a moment they faded to twitching, and then the ant was still.

The spider spooled greasy thread from its rear and transformed the ant into a tightly-wrapped cocoon. Its companion wove a similar casket for the second.

As I let Li down off my shoulders, the third ant bucked and clacked its pincers. Sheer will or an act of God allowed it to tear itself free, and it tumbled fifteen feet to the ground.

Time slowed.

The ant lumbered in our direction, two legs still bound with silk. The spiders plopped down after it.

Zip dove left. Li and I flung ourselves right. The ant brushed between us and plummeted through the floor, dragging a good portion of the clearing with it. The first spider flew after it. Like bystanders during a bank robbery, we tried to make ourselves as small as possible.

The second spider paused at the edge of the new-formed pit. Its abdomen swelled and contracted. While it considered a descent, it noticed Li and me crouched beside the obelisk.

Li let loose with the SCAR, stitching a path of bullets from its eye-cluttered face down the length of its abdomen. On the other side of the pit, Zip unloaded his handgun.

For a moment the spider wavered, four of its legs pulling it towards Li, the others reaching for Zip. It settled on us, but we were already seeking cover in a thicket. Meanwhile, Zip emptied another magazine, and the spider wheeled to face the hail of bullets.

Zip scrambled up a tree trunk. At full speed, the spider could have plucked him off the bark like a grape, but another barrage from the SCAR and my own pistol kept it off balance.

The climb was nothing for Zip. I'd seen him scale a glass office building just to impress a girl. By the time the spider reached the base of the tree, he was well out of reach.

Then he fucked up. He could have kept climbing and grapple-gunned to safety, but instead he stepped onto a branch directly above the spider and fired six shots into its chitinous head.

The spider rammed into the tree, sending shivers up the trunk, and Zip's branch gave way with a groan, dropping onto the spider's upward-gaping maw—

A pincer boomeranged across the clearing, trailing goopy black bile. Zip threw himself free and rolled to a stop at the edge of the pit. Again Li's SCAR roared.

The spider staggered, orange goo gushing from a dozen spouts. As it floundered away, a leg lashed out, catching Zip full in the chest—

For a moment he floated in midair, eyes as wide and disbelieving as Junior's had been. Then he was gone, hurled unceremoniously into the abyss, and blood pumped thick and heavy through the red corridors of my skull.

9

Zip's parents hated each other, but, for religious reasons, they refused to get a divorce. They also refused to use birth control. It wasn't a great combination. Zip was their fifth child, and by that point they'd quit even trying to come up with names, which is how he wound up Zachary Taylor Chase.

"The most fucked up thing in my childhood was the way we went through pets," Zip told me once at Thai Restaurant, our favorite Thai restaurant. Palm-sized silver fish swam fin-to-fin in an endless slow arc around an aquarium beside us.

"My dad spent most of his time at work," said Zip. "There, or the bar, or his girlfriend's place. Avoided our house like it was radioactive."

I'd skipped breakfast that morning, and my stomach was beginning to turn on itself.

"He sounds like a piece of shit," I said.

"That's what he was afraid we'd think," said Zip, "so he kept bringing home puppies. For the optics."

I sipped my water.

"My mom hated that," said Zip. "She was already raising six kids by herself, and she didn't like animals to begin with. Plus these dogs were a representation of my dad. Three of them ran away, two got hit by cars, and another one died in our backyard because she refused to take him to the vet."

"He could at least have gotten you fish, or something."

"Oh, he did. We had fish for a while. Keeping them alive is impossible, though."

"Can't be that hard."

"Don't feed a fish for a couple of days and it'll die. But if you feed it too much, that'll kill it too."

"Like the pandas at the zoo. The ones they can't convince to mate. Isn't evolution supposed to weed that out?"

"I don't think fish even want to be alive," said Zip. "If the water's too cold, too hot, too blue, too wet—any excuse they find, they'll pounce on it and die, and then when you find them floating at the top of the tank they give you that look, like it's your fault—"

He puffed his cheeks, widened his eyes, and furrowed his eyebrows.

"That's good," I said. "That's a reproachful fish, right there."

Zip bought a pug puppy when his first paycheck came through. His apartment didn't even have furniture. He was sleeping on a pile of blankets. Getting a dog was priority number one.

He named the puppy Chomper. Chomper was a big fan of me, so much so that he lost control of his bladder every time I visited. At first Zip found this hilarious, but by the sixth or seventh time he was exasperated.

"Can we stop coming to my place?" he said, grabbing paper towels off the fridge.

"Your TV's bigger," I said. Chomper was running figure eights through my legs, so I leaned down to scratch him behind the ears.

"You're a good boy," I said. His little pink tongue drooped happily out of his mouth.

"Don't say that," said Zip, mopping. "Don't tell him that."

Even Li liked Chomper, and she hated dogs.

Whenever Zip went on an expedition, he left Chomper with his sister. The worst part of watching him vanish into the pit was knowing that he'd never retrieve his dog.

The darkness yawned.

"We're going after him," I said.

"No shit," said Li.

A few months earlier I'd run into Sergeant Rivers at a bar near RangerCorp headquarters. After a few drinks I asked if he thought he'd made the right decision by trying to save his partner. He tightened his lips and rubbed the rim of his empty eye socket.

"The smart thing to do," he said, "is not always the right thing to do."

Side by side, Li and I rappelled into the abyss.

10

The pit was cool and dark and bottomless. There was no trace of the ant or the spider. Perhaps the ant still fled, somewhere far below, the spider trailing frothing ribbons of drool a few feet behind.

The firepower we'd unloaded on the surface had not gone unnoticed. Furious cries barraged us as we sank through the soupy gloom. Our headlamps painted rolling ovals across the forest's tangled brown skeleton.

How long would we look before giving up? The thought provoked a whiplash of guilt. What kind of friend was I? But if he'd fallen far enough, there wouldn't be any point in finding him. It didn't make sense for us to die too, did it?

If only we'd listened to him and left. If only the branch had held. If only the spider's leg hadn't happened to find him. Was the barrier between life and death really that thin?

Li whistled. She'd found Zip's body on a ledge protruding from one of the earthy walls. I willed him to turn and look up at us, give a toothy grin, but his body remained still.

Something hairy was clambering up from the depths. Through the decaying infrastructure, I glimpsed matted fur and long gray fingers with multiple joints. Fingers thicker than telephone poles snaked around branches and outcroppings as the beast hauled itself upward.

"Go," said Li, planting both feet against me and exploding away. I swung toward Zip, flicking the grapple gun to allow more line to flow. I left enough slack to land on the ledge with room to spare, but the edge gave way beneath my feet, sending dirt and half-eaten wood spiraling down while I scrabbled for purchase.

Zip remained inert as I reached his side. Dozens of hand-sized insects leapt off his body, fleeing my headlamp. There was no time to check his pulse. I hooked his belt to my line and hefted him over my shoulder.

The ascending beast unleashed a guttural roar. It was an ape with dull black eyes and a mouth that sucked in a roomful of air with each breath. Tree trunks gave way before it like rotten toothpicks.

I tripped a button on the grapple gun and began to rise. A spider crawled out from under Zip's shirt and onto my neck, leaping away before I could bring my hand around to swat it. The sensation of legs prickling my skin remained.

The SCAR crashed and spat. Li, twenty feet above and ascending rapidly, sprayed at flies burrowing out of the opposite wall. The flies were translucent, like rice paper, with bright red eyes and convoluted organs. One leapt into space and clasped itself around Li's legs. The proboscis prepared to plunge into her stomach—

Calmly, almost casually, Li jammed the barrel of the SCAR against the insect's head and fired. The fly exploded, drenching her in fluid, and the jittering limbs released her. I watched the segmented body tumble past. The ape snagged it out of the air and tossed it down its gullet.

Grunts and roars merged with buzzing flies and the throaty voice of the SCAR to form a clobbering wall of sound. I fired into the maelstrom as the surface neared. The insects seemed reluctant to pounce, but greedy enough that they didn't want to leave us alone, even as more of them crumpled under the flood of hot lead. When Li vanished over the edge, the swarm followed. My line whizzed me up and over. Li helped me to my feet. We unhooked ourselves from the grapple guns—no time to unwind the hooks—and blitzed across the clearing toward the spider web. Zip bounced, heavy and limp, on my shoulder.

Knocked out of the air by one of its fellows, a fly thwacked against me. I struck out and felt delicate exoskeleton crunch. My fist came away soaking wet.

The ape fought through the aperture in the floor, bellowing.

We slid under the web and ran hard. With no grapple guns to carry us into the branches, we had to find another kind of cover. Flies whapped like baseballs against the web, tangling themselves in the thick silk. I glanced back and saw what looked like hundreds of the fat insects trapped, roiling, and then the ape bulled full-speed into them, tearing a path with its ferocious hands.

The ape's incisors gleamed when it roared. It wrenched the web away from its face to fix hideous eyes upon us. The web, lumpy with flies, trailed after it like a demented wedding dress.

A third spider, larger than the previous two, fell out of the trees and blocked our way. We cut left, but the spider wasn't interested in us. Furious at the destruction of its web, it leapt toward the ape, wrapping around the beast's hulking arm and plunging fangs into the thick, muscular shoulder.

The ape spun. I tackled Li as the cape of fly-filled spider web whipped just overhead. As we rose, the ape yanked the spider off its arm and spiked it into the ground. Then, looming tall, it spread its hands apart—

The merciless palms closed with a thunderclap on the spider's swollen abdomen, which popped like a kickball in a trash compactor. Orange-red juices spurted everywhere, spattering our necks with foul-smelling drops. The ape set to work tearing the legs off, stuffing them into its mouth as the spider screamed and writhed. A descending gray fist crushed the head and stilled the twitching pincers.

Li and I reached the place where our hooks were secured and hastened to free them. Moments later we were soaring up to safety and the sweet smell of clean canopy air.

We swung from tree to tree, dodging creatures that dive-bombed the opposite direction, until finally we reached a place where the forest was quiet, and the canopy still, and we laid Zip down to find that breath still came, measured and slow and strong, through his corrugated lips.

11

Zip's left leg was broken. It was purple and lumpy and when he woke the first thing he did was sit up and try to touch it. That's when we realized he had a broken rib, too, because as fast as he'd sat up, he flapped back down again.

"Oh, fuck," he said. "My ribs —"

We unzipped his jacket and pulled up his shirt. His chest was a patchwork of bruises.

"My leg," he said. "Oh, fuck, guys, I'm dead. I'm so fucking dead."

"You're going to be fine," said Li.

"We're twelve days in," said Zip. "You can't get me out."

"Yes we can."

"Listen to yourself."

"You can walk."

"My leg's splinters. I can't fucking walk."

"We'll make crutches."

Zip's face was drawn tight over his cheekbones. It made me uncomfortable to look at him. I scanned the canopy and tried not to think about what a broken leg meant in the forest. Sometimes even a sprained ankle was enough.

"I'm not letting you die," said Li.

"Tetris," said Zip, "you gotta take care of Chomper, okay? Can you promise me that?"

I dug at the grime under my fingernails. I had dirt and dried insect blood everywhere—the corners of my eyes, the creases in my palms, the sweaty crevices in my joints—but it was thickest under my nails.

"I don't care if I have to carry you over my shoulder the whole way," I said. "We're taking you home."

Zip let his head fall back.

"You're welcome, by the way," said Li. "We fought King Kong for you, stud."

Zip moaned. We gave him ibuprofen capsules.

"You need a splint," said Li.

"I need a lot of things," said Zip.

Li and I gathered sticks. We wrapped the leg with bandages, then strapped on the splint.

"Fixed," I said, and Zip almost smiled.

Night came quickly. I dreamed I was back at my brother's viewing, the casket open, but instead of Todd it was Zip lying stone-faced inside. A second Zip stood beside me, examining the corpse with an undertaker's eye.

"Top-notch embalming," said the living Zip. "Looks like I'm just asleep."

In the morning Zip's eyes seemed to have receded back into his skull, and his teeth were clenched together, but he'd regained a bit of his normal cheer.

"If we make it out of here, I'm getting a bright pink cast," he said.

"That'll suit you, I think."

"Women love an injured man. This may turn out to be a net positive."

He leaned on me as we trudged along. I had to hunch so he could put his arm around my neck. Soon my spine was on fire.

"I'm just glad it was me and not you," said Zip. "There's no way I could carry your fat ass."

"Runt like you? Of course not."

Not since my earliest expeditions had I felt so vulnerable on the forest floor. If something jumped out at us, I'd have to swing Zip across my shoulders and make a run for it, which in most cases would be an exercise in futility. The pressure on Li was tremendous, too, because she had to keep watch all by herself. But this was Li we were talking about. All day long, she threaded us around ravines, trap doors and sink holes, lithe and sure-footed, a panther with two stumbling cubs in tow.

We pushed hard, but it was like wading through pudding, and after three days we'd only made two days of progress.

"This is going to take forever," observed Zip as we settled in for the third evening. "We're going to run out of food."

"So we skip dinners," said Li. "Starting tonight. The food will last."

We slept with our stomachs pinching. In the morning, the breakfast bars and gel packets hardly seemed a meal. I wished for a stack of pancakes and a sheaf of bacon strips. And fast food hash browns, the kind I ate on road trips as a kid. All of it steaming on a shining platter in front of me.

On the fourth day we crossed paths with a herd of pill bugs. We hauled ass into a tree and watched them pass.

Forest pill bugs had the bulk and personality of terrestrial cattle. They grazed on whatever they passed, and wouldn't hurt you unless you went to spectacular lengths to piss them off. When confronted by a predator, they curled into armored balls and scattered like a handful of flung marbles.

Zip leaned against the trunk with his eyes closed. His face was linen-white and drawn.

I nudged him. "You doing okay?"

Zip remained silent.

"Looks like it's time for more ibuprofen," said Li.

"Morphine, please," said Zip.

"Not yet," said Li.

Zip looked like he was settling in for a nap. Li scooted closer to me.

"It's going to get worse," she whispered in my ear. "Every step he takes, the broken edges are grinding on each other."

She made her hands into fists and rubbed the knuckles against each other.

Her face was grimy and smeared. It was also painfully

beautiful. I wanted to cradle her head and put my thumbs on her cheeks and wipe away the dirt. I wanted to kiss her on her tight-pressed lips. She was right there! Zip was half-asleep. I could do it. Lean in and kiss her. I wanted...

I whipped my head away. No. What the fuck was that?

Zip was dying. This was not the time to entertain adolescent fantasies. Li had made it abundantly clear that she wasn't interested in me. I had to crush that feeling, throw it down a mineshaft and bury it with concrete.

Li waved a hand in front of my face. "Hello?"

Below, the pillbugs stripped the forest floor clean, mouthparts milling industriously.

A few nights later I dreamed myself back to my dad's house in Indianapolis. I was sipping a glass of lemonade on the porch. Hollywood was there too. He sprawled on a lawn chair with a hat pulled low over his eyes. Only his jaw moved, grinding away at a lump of bubble gum.

The sky hung low and red and empty. No clouds, no sun, just the dull, uniform color of congealing blood.

"You should listen to him, you know," said Hollywood, chewing his gum.

I peered at the red sky. "Who?"

Then a scorpion began to clamber over the white picket fence, and I wrenched myself awake.

My sleeping bag was sticky with sweat. I tried to chase the nightmare away with memories of home: bright summer days at the court by the public pool, heat radiating pleasantly off the blacktop, the rubber-and-leather smell of the basketball transferring to my palms.

Shockingly clean sneakers with soft, fat laces.

Clean shoes sounded amazing. Socks, too. We'd reached the stage of the expedition when rotating between three pairs no longer kept them remotely fresh. Grime had infiltrated every crevice of my body, causing a perpetual, slow-burning itch. I would have traded half my expedition payout for a shower.

Sleep, when it returned, was torn jagged by rapid-fire dreams in which I ran or climbed or flew, fleeing something I was afraid to turn and glimpse.

The next morning was dim and gloomy. Nobody felt like talking. We downed our food bars and continued the trek, obsessively checking our compasses to make sure we were heading as close to due east as possible.

Zip pulled further and further into himself. I dragged him along, and his legs moved, but his mind was miles away. He never asked for painkillers, so we kept an eye on his jaw, and when he clenched it harder than usual we knew it was time to administer another dose.

Around lunch we came across the body of a subway snake. It was rare to see one on the surface. This one must have thrashed furiously when it died, because a wide swath around its corpse was scraped clear of vegetation. Its ridged body curved and rolled out of sight like a levee tracing the edge of a tortuous river. The tip of the tail might have been half a mile away.

The snake's mouth gaped, a cave bristling with serrated teeth, the heavy jaw dislocated. Jettisoned from the mouth, in a puddle of snake vomit, was the half-digested corpse of a giant blue frog. Even for an animal as large as the snake, the toxin coating the frog's skin would have proved lethal in minutes.

The three of us stood, transfixed, imagining the snake in motion. Thousands of tons of scales and muscle, rippling in tune. It must have downed a mountain of meat every day. How else could it keep its ravenous bulk satisfied?

"What a shame," said Li.

Out of nothingness this gigantic creature had grown, a universe of trillions and trillions of cells, over decades, maybe even centuries, and the whole system had collapsed one day because it took a bite out of the wrong frog. Now scavengers would clean it down to the bone. A shining white skeleton would be all that remained, and then the forest would swallow that too.

The snake's skin swelled and we stumbled back, fearing that breath had returned to its mighty lungs. Instead a centipede burst through the thick hide, sniffing the air with its antennae. Out of the gap poured an odor so foul that my breakfast began to rise up my throat.

"Wonderful," I said, and spat.

As we turned to leave, skin wriggled all down the side of the snake. The scavengers were already hard at work.

Late one afternoon, as the forest began to dim, we heard a woman scream.

"Don't go chasing after that, now," said Li.

I smiled. "I believe that's the first joke anybody's told in a week."

"Face it, guys," said Zip, quiet and gravelly. "I'm the funny one. Without me you're boring."

"Well, yeah," said Li. "Why do you think we're trying so hard to save you?"

That night it rained and rained. In the morning Zip moaned and refused to move. We checked his splint and saw that the wrappings were soaked through with blood. As we unwrapped his leg, a sickening smell assaulted us. A spear of bone had punctured the skin of his calf. The whole area was lurid, yellow and red, and humming with infection.

We slathered the wound with antiseptics and bandaged it carefully. While Li put together a stretcher, I managed to get Zip to swallow some antibiotics, along with a few gulps of water.

Off we went, Zip strapped to the stretcher between us, four or five days from shore. If we were lucky, we could make it there in three.

12

At first, the jostling of the stretcher was enough to keep Zip awake. He was even alert enough to spot a flesh wasp and croak at us to get down. But the next day he hardly opened his eyes, and the day after that, we couldn't wake him up. His forehead was aflame.

"Trees look like they're thinning out to you?" I asked, lifting the stretcher over a fallen branch.

"Yeah," said Li, "yeah, we're almost there. Today, I think."

"Today," I repeated. I could feel the forest laughing at us.

By the evening we were close. The trees grew smaller, the canopy hanging lower and less dense overhead. There were even a few gaps in the leaves, puzzle pieces of darkening sky. Soon it would be night.

Without discussing it, Li and I came to the same conclusion. We weren't stopping. We flicked our headlamps on and increased our pace as much as we dared.

"Time to radio for pickup?"

"We can't," said Li. "They can't know we're back."

"Zip's going to die," I said.

"I'll call 911 on my cell," said Li. "As soon as I've got service."

I grimaced but didn't argue. If we were truly uncovering some insidious government conspiracy, falling into their hands would put all three of our lives in danger. But waiting for cell coverage instead of using the radio would push back our call until we were only a few minutes from shore.

So, the new plan: call 911. Sneak back to civilization in the ambulance, set Zip up in a hospital, then bolt for the nearest internet-equipped PC to post our footage. Hollywood lived in San Diego. Maybe he'd help. Although something told me he wouldn't be interested in involving himself.

Our ranger careers were finished. We were breaking six contract clauses and a handful of federal laws. The lawyers would say we were putting Zip's life in danger, stealing expedition footage and releasing it outside the company's channels for personal gain. At best, Li and I were headed for jail. At worst, the government would find a way to make us disappear.

Walking through the forest at night made the hair on my arms stand up. Darkness pressed in on the cone of light from my headlamp. I tried not to think about the predators that could be stalking us, lurking just out of sight. The list was long. But we had to be close to the shore.

After a while, Li paused. We put down the stretcher and she rooted through her pack for her phone.

"One bar," she whispered triumphantly, flashing the screen my way. She dialed 911.

"Hi, we need an ambulance along the shoreline south of San Diego," said Li, keeping her voice low and flicking her beam around the clearing. "We're coming out of the forest with a critically injured person."

The darkness rustled and trilled as Li listened to the voice on the other end.

"No, I don't have a more precise location," she said. "Get rolling and I'll call when we're out."

Something trumpeted. The ground shook. Li shut the phone, yanked up her end of the stretcher, and ran. I struggled to keep track of the ground beneath my feet, scarcely avoiding tripping over the branches and vines that zipped into view.

We ran for a long time, until red daggers filled my lungs. At last the trumpeting grew distant, as whatever had chased us gave up or found more promising prey. We kept running: the trees ended up ahead. The incandescent eyes of a Coast Guard tower glimmered through the leaves.

As we stood, blinking and gasping, under the floodlights, an ambulance came barreling down the slope, trailed by several unmarked black vans.

Li ripped off her headlamp and ran a hand through her close-cropped hair.

"They already know," she said.

In a moment we were encircled. Out of the ambulance sprang paramedics, who rushed to Zip and transferred him onto a stretcher of their own. Out of the vans came a dozen men in bulky black body armor. They trained their rifles on us as the paramedics wheeled Zip away.

"Drop your weapons," shouted one of the soldiers, and we obliged, tossing them into a pile: the SCAR, the pistols, and the grapple guns. Li slung her pack to the ground, and I followed suit, rolling my aching shoulders.

"Easy," I said.

"Hands on your head," screamed the soldier.

Too tired to protest, I lifted my grimy hands and rested them atop my head. Li crossed her arms across her chest and glared. Looking at her, I dropped my arms back to my sides.

"I said hands on your heads!"

"That's enough," said Agent Cooper, stepping out of the rightmost van. "They're cooperating. Stand down."

His smile was uncomfortably wide, and I expected a slim tongue to come flickering through the teeth.

"Welcome back," said Cooper. "We'll take care of Mr. Chase. But you two are coming with me."

13

Cooper sat across from us in the back of the van with the smile still plastered across his face. After a while he donned a pair of sunglasses. Li curled and uncurled her fingers, sometimes cracking the knuckles. I reclined with hands on my knees. Why hadn't they handcuffed us? Didn't they know what we were?

I eyed the soldier next to me. His head was a boulder perched atop mountainous shoulders. There was a comparatively tiny pistol in a holster at his side. I could grab the gun before he could react, put an incapacitating round in his knee cap, turn, and drop the other guard. Li would pick up on the plan as soon as I moved. She'd lunge across the aisle, knock Cooper out, and move on to the soldiers who flanked him—but then what? And what if something went wrong? What if we had to kill someone?

That's what Cooper was counting on. We weren't murderers.

Still, the lack of respect irked me. I'd like to see these thugs survive three days in the forest, weighed down by bulky body armor and assault rifles. The vests might stop bullets, but foot-long teeth would slice through them like lasers through tissue paper.

In the 80s the US Army tried sending a full battalion of soldiers into the forest. These were the best of the best: steely killing machines, bristling with the most fearsome weaponry available. For the first time, it was thought, military technology would give mankind a fighting chance against the denizens of the forest. This was the experiment. High-caliber automatic weapons, armor-piercing rounds, shoulder-mounted rocket launchers, flamethrowers that spewed their searing payload a hundred yards—how could anything composed of mere flesh and bone withstand such an assault?

Dutifully, in a nod to the experts who counseled vigorously against any excursion of this size, the battalion was accompanied by five ranger guides.

At first, the expedition met little resistance. Flesh wasps and other airborne creatures were terminated on sight, reduced to bloody globs by shoulder-mounted missiles. Spider burrows were identified and cleared with grenades. Raising everyone's spirits, a marauding subway snake was brought low by blistering fire from machine guns and rocket launchers. Minimal casualties were sustained.

By the fourth night, the battalion had fallen into a routine. After making camp, the soldiers would set up a perimeter of floodlights, leaving a full quarter of their number on watch at any given time. Around this bubble of light, the forest roiled and screamed, but anything that ventured inside was driven back by a flood of lead.

The soldiers began to feel safe. They grew confident, no longer fearing the titanic creatures that gnashed their teeth in the darkness.

But the forest had not given up. Insistently, it probed the contours of the bubble the men had constructed. It knew that they were most vulnerable at night. Men had to sleep. The forest did not.

Deep in the fourth night, as the lookouts' eyelids grew heavy, the forest struck.

An oval of floor beneath the sleeping soldiers crumbled away, revealing a leviathan all serrated teeth and yawning gullet. Half a company was lost at once, sucked into the whizzing rows of teeth. As the creature flopped its hideous mass higher, foul cyclone breath washing over the bubble, a second assault was launched. A thousand spiders, screeching in unison, rushed down the trees and fell upon the scattered soldiers.

The noise must have been terrific. Suddenly it was every man for himself, and all military discipline was forgotten. Muzzle flash lit the clearing in lieu of the overturned floodlights, and flamethrowers wielded in panicked disarray set vegetation and piled carcasses alight.

As the defensive perimeter crumbled, new predators came stampeding in from all sides, elbowing their way into the bloodshed.

To their credit, some of the soldiers weathered the storm, collapsing inward into a core so dense and tight and well-armed that it could not be breached. If the fearsome creatures had worked together, these remaining humans would have been swiftly devoured, but once the battle was underway the forest turned on itself. The humans crept away, and when morning came the light revealed that thirty had survived. Among them: three of the five rangers.

Licking their wounds, the survivors headed for shore. Without a battalion's full firepower to deter them, guerilla predators nipped at the party from all sides—a trapdoor spider snatching one man and vanishing into its tunnels, a blood bat descending silently and soaring back to the canopy with human prey in its talons—and the nights were fraught with terror.

Of the nine hundred men who entered the forest, only two survived.

The van rolled to a bumpy stop.

"Get out," said Cooper.

We stepped into an empty parking lot beside a long, squat building. Towering floodlights bombarded us with artificial light. The brightness hurt my eyes. The building only seemed to have one floor, but its footprint was enormous, the corners far away in the distance. There were no windows.

Taking his time, Cooper stepped out the back of the van and sank his hands into his pockets.

"Come on," he said, and motioned with his chin.

"No," said Li. She planted her muddy boots on the asphalt. "We're not going anywhere until we get some answers."

Cooper was inscrutable behind his sunglasses. "You'll get your answers. Inside."

"Fuck you."

He sighed and brushed dust from his suit jacket.

"I'm not the bad guy," he said. "Which, I realize, is what the bad guy would say. But I'm saying it nonetheless."

They ended up having to handcuff us after all.

14

In a gray, windowless room, with uncovered light bulbs beating down, Li and I waited for Agent Cooper to return.

"I hope he brings cheeseburgers," said Li.

Our handcuffs were linked to the table through steel loops.

"They questioned me and Hollywood in a room like this," I said.

Li didn't reply.

I'd last seen Hollywood in a San Diego dive bar. I arrived just as the biggest dude in the place smashed a barstool over his blond head. As the whole establishment descended into bedlam, I dragged Hollywood out the door and a respectable distance down the street. In return I received a drunken wallop in the eye.

"This is why nobody likes you," I said as I staggered away.

He wrapped himself around a telephone pole like it was the only stationary object on Earth.

"Hey, Tetris, you know what?" he said as his head lolled to the side.

"What?"

"Go fuck yourself."

Agent Cooper came through the door with an enormous paper bag cradled in his arms.

"Not quite cheeseburgers," he said. "There's a great Indian place around the corner. Gimme a sec, I'll grab some plates."

He placed the bag on the table and left. Li stretched against the handcuffs and managed to tug the food over. Rooting through, she laid each dish on the table. Despite myself, I was pleased. Indian food was my second-favorite cuisine. It dawned on me that Cooper probably knew that.

"They have us under surveillance all the time, you think?" I asked.

"Motherfucker even knew our orders," said Li. "Chicken korma, vegetable pakoras, lamb biriyani. No mango lassi, though. Good thing Zip's not here. He'd throw a fit."

We munched on the pakoras while we waited. They were the crispy kind: my favorite.

The door was ajar. I considered the odds of a successful escape. Even if we got out of the handcuffs, we'd passed countless security checkpoints on the way down. Still, it seemed sloppy to leave that door open. A play to make us feel at ease?

"Sorry about that," said Cooper when he returned. "Break room was out of plates. Had to run up a floor."

He unlocked our handcuffs and stacked them, then leaned back and watched us tear into the food.

"Not polite to stare at somebody when they're eating," said Li with her mouth full. "Your mother never teach you manners?"

Cooper smiled. "She certainly tried."

"Where'd you take Zip?" I asked, wiping my mouth.

"Hospital in San Diego," said Cooper. "He should be alright."

The food was delicious. I had to force myself to slow down. Gorging yourself after an expedition was a great way to land a crippling stomachache.

"I'm sure you have more questions than that," said Cooper.

Li wiped her fingers one at a time.

"I'll try to fill in some blanks," said Cooper. "First: those body cameras don't just record."

"Yeah, no, that's pretty obvious, now," said Li.

"Signal can only reach us when you're fifty miles from shore, but that still gives us plenty of time to screen the footage before you arrive."

"You knew about the monolith," I said. "You knew about the tablet, about what LaMonte saw, everything."

Cooper nodded. "Yuuup."

"Why cover it up?"

He leaned across the table. "Time for some game theory."

Li snorted.

"Let's say we knew there was something in there," said Cooper. "Something big and scary. An entity we didn't fully understand. What would we do?"

"Warn everyone," said Li. "And then kill it."

"Come on. Would we want to advertise its presence to the world? Would we want to get everybody riled up before we fully understood what it was, and what it wanted, and what it was capable of?"

He seemed to be waiting for a response, and I enjoyed refusing to give him one.

"No, we would not," said Cooper. "We would not want that. It would cause panic. More importantly, from a strategic perspective, it would tell the thing in the forest—the entity, the civilization, whatever it was—it would tell it that we knew it was there."

"People have a right to know," said Li.

Cooper laughed uproariously.

"Oh, that's a good one," he said, wiping the corner of his eye. "That's one of my favorites."

"So the whole ranger program is fake?" I asked.

Cooper slowly regained his composure. "Well, rangers would probably have developed anyway. But yes, we use it as a sort of camouflage. You're not just filming television. You're also gathering intelligence."

"So what's in there?" asked Li. "What are we dealing with?"

"When you're finished eating," said Cooper, "I'll take you to someone who can tell you everything we know."

We followed Cooper into an elevator and he hit the lowest button. The elevator hummed as it plummeted. Cooper's suit was immaculate, well-pressed, pin-striped, and perfectly tailored to his slight frame. Beside him, Li was coated in grime, mud caked on her boots up to the ankles. Her face was dark with dirt. Both of us left clods of dried mud and brown smears everywhere we went.

"No guards this time?" asked Li. "Guess you figured out they wouldn't be much help."

"I wouldn't be so sure about that," said Cooper, straightening his tie.

"You don't give rangers enough credit," I said. "Just because those guys are bigger doesn't mean they're more dangerous."

Cooper examined me, eyes half-lidded.

"You're more cocky than I remembered," he said. "I thought Rivers was supposed to beat that out of you."

"Just honest," I said.

"The big gentleman beside you in the van? He was a POW for a week or two in Afghanistan," said Cooper. "When they tried to interrogate him, he snapped the restraints."

"Strong dude," I said. "I get it."

"They shot him four times, point blank. Two in the shoulder, two in the gut. He killed eight of them with his bare hands."

Li shifted her weight to the other foot.

"After that he had a weapon. Escape from the camp was easy. But he had to cross the desert, walk a hundred miles, with no food and only the water he could carry."

The elevator jolted to a stop. With an airy ding, the doors parted.

"I'm not saying you don't have a hard job," said Cooper.

"Just that you're not the only ones."

He took us through a maze of corridors, finally stopping before a pair of double doors.

"Try to behave," he said, and pushed them open.

On the other side was an enormous pit of a room with descending tiers connected by waffled steel steps. Complex machinery chimed and blinked. In the center, at a table with a hologram projected above it, stood a woman in a white lab coat with hair past her shoulders.

"Hey, Coop," she said. "Who are they?"

She spoke quietly, but somehow her voice still reached us. Cooper trotted down the steps.

"Rangers," he said.

"I can see that," said the woman. "They're going to get dirt everywhere."

She wasn't wrong. You could trace our progress by the debris we left behind.

"Sorry about that, ma'am," I said.

"This is Doctor Alvarez," said Cooper. "She's the best we've got."

"Try not to touch anything," said Dr. Alvarez.

Li walked around the table, examining the hologram, which depicted a slowly-twirling molecule. Dr. Alvarez wore a thin glove with blue spots on the fingers. When she motioned with the gloved hand, the hologram shrank and vanished.

"You're too young to be a doctor," said Li.

"Apparently not. What are you here for?"

"The forest," said Cooper. "Tell them everything."

"Everything?"

Cooper spread his arms and beamed. "Everything."

Dr. Alvarez tapped a few keystrokes and a green globe materialized overhead.

"The Earth," said Dr. Alvarez. "Familiar enough. Continents. The World Forest. Past certain latitudes, the polar wastes."

As she spoke, she twisted the gloved hand, and the globe rotated accordingly.

"Can either of you tell me how life on Earth originated?"

I looked at Li. Science hadn't been my best subject. To be fair, I hadn't really paid attention in any of my subjects.

"Single-celled organisms in lakes," said Li.

"Close, but wrong," said Dr. Alvarez.

Li furrowed her brow. "Wait a minute."

"That's what they teach you in school," said Dr. Alvarez, "but I assure you: it's wrong."

A few more keystrokes and the Earth was replaced by a blue globe with a single gigantic continent in the middle.

"This is the Earth," said Dr. Alvarez, "one billion years ago."

I watched the globe as it spun. "What's all the blue?"

"Water," said Dr. Alvarez.

My head thumped. The blue orb slowly turned.

"Where's the forest?"

"Exactly," said Dr. Alvarez.

Li tugged her earlobe. "You're telling me the whole planet used to be one huge lake?"

"They're called oceans," said Dr. Alvarez, "from the Greek 'okeanos,' meaning 'great river.' It's there, in the oceans, that life on Earth began."

I was suddenly very tired. I looked for a place to sit down, but everything was covered in blinking buttons and dials.

"How do you know?" asked Li.

"Geological records," said Dr. Alvarez. "Until about sixty-five million years ago, seventy percent of the Earth's surface was covered by water. After that? No more oceans. Instead, forest."

She tapped a few more keystrokes. "The World Forest is not natural. It's not supposed to be there."

The globe morphed once again. Now I recognized the outlines of the modern continents, but instead of the forest and white-brown polar wastes, these continents were surrounded by dazzling blue.

"That's what the world is supposed to look like," said Dr. Alvarez, with just the slightest hint of sadness.

I couldn't comprehend that much water. Couldn't even picture it. Whole continents of water. You could swim for years and never make it across.

"Something, or someone, put the forest there," said Dr. Alvarez. "And it's our job to figure out why."

15

After a while my eyelids started getting heavy and I could no longer keep track of what Dr. Alvarez was saying. My mind would wander away mid-sentence, and when it returned she'd be firing off incomprehensible multisyllabic words.

Dr. Alvarez caught me yawning. "You going to let these kids sleep?"

Cooper jumped.

"Oh, yeah," he said. "C'mon, I'll show you to your room."

"You're not letting us go?" asked Li.

"It's not like that," said Cooper. "We've got something to discuss tomorrow. We could put you up in a hotel, but there are perfectly comfortable accommodations within the facility."

Perfectly comfortable accommodations turned out to be a cold concrete room with two cots and a yellowing bathroom.

"This is going to earn you a one-star review on TripGuide," said Li.

"Very funny," said Cooper. "There's a call button on the wall if you need anything. I'll send fresh clothes down. Soap and toiletries are in the bathroom."

"Dibs on the first shower," said Li. I winced. The floor would be a muddy mess by the time I got my turn.

"Do you give this tour to all the rangers?" I asked.

Cooper paused in the doorway. "You think this happens to everybody?"

"Finding spooky shit? Happened to me twice already."

"Not to inflate your already cumbersome ego by implying that you're special, but this is a once-in-a-decade occurrence. The vast majority of rangers go their entire career without finding anything."

I tried to read his face, but as usual it was illegible behind bland corporate geniality.

"Get the clothes," said Li. "If you need me, I'll be checking the shower for cameras."

After Cooper left, I followed her into the bathroom, where she was scouring the ceiling.

"Find anything?"

"Nope," she said. "Probably bugs in the vents, though."

"Do you believe him?"

"About what?"

"That nobody ever finds anything in the forest?"

"Sure. Maybe."

She balanced on the rim of the tub, examining the rings holding up the shower curtain.

"Isn't it weird, then? That I found it twice?"

She laughed. "What do you want me to say? You're the chosen one?"

"It just creeps me out, is all."

Li hopped down and put a hand on my shoulder.

"Look," she said, "we have no reason to think they're being honest. They're putting on an act, all this buddy-buddy shit, trying to make us feel like part of their fucked-up team. I'm not buying it."

After a few seconds withering in her raptor gaze, I nodded.

"That's what I'm worried about right now," said Li. "That and Zip. Fuck the tablet. I don't care anymore. I just want to know that we're getting out of here, and that Zip's alive."

While she showered I had another crisis of willpower, imagining her stripped bare, the hot water steaming off her skin. I thought about going to the door, asking—did she mind if I joined her?

Stupid.

When she finally emerged, wrapped in a towel, her legs clean and wet and exposed, something must have shown in my expression.

"What?" she said.

I planted my eyes on her face. "Umm."

"Oh. I get it."

"Nothing," I said. "Sorry. No. I mean, no. Not that."

"Am I going to be safe sleeping in the same room as you?"

"I have no idea what you're talking about."

She laughed. "Your turn, bud. Believe I used up all the hot water."

She hadn't, of course. It was like a hotel: you could stay in there for hours and the heat would never fade. I closed my eyes and let my skin turn red. The first shower after an expedition, I always cranked the heat up until it hurt, because the dirt and toxins of the forest had worked their way deep into my pores. I had to roast myself, all the grime and dead skin peeling away, and emerge like a molting lizard with a fresh new exterior.

Li was already asleep when I finished. Her eyes were closed, her mouth ajar. For a minute or two I stood there looking at her. Then I shook myself and finished toweling off.

I was unconscious within seconds of slipping under the covers.

In the middle of the night I heard a noise and woke up. Li wasn't in her bed. Her empty sheets were pulled aside, tangled. Light trickled around the edges of the bathroom door. The fan whined insistently.

"You alright in there?" I called.

Nothing. I waited a few seconds. Still no response. She probably couldn't hear me over the fan.

Back in my apartment, I sometimes spent nights staring at the dark rectangle of my bedroom doorway, imagining what'd I'd do if someone—something?—glided into view. Something tall. Something even darker than the black rectangle out of which it emerged, except for a glistening mouth. The fear made no sense. But maybe that was the problem: to make a rational judgment about the safety of your surroundings, you needed sensory data, which darkness denied.

When I listened closely, I thought I heard a tapping sound. I held my breath and inclined my head, trying to locate the source. It was probably a pipe, or something to do with the air conditioning. I had noises like this back in my apartment complex. I closed my eyes and tried to sleep.

Tap. Tap tap. Tap tap tap.

The bathroom door slammed open, and I sat up to look. It was Junior, eyes a coruscant black, with blood positively gushing from his mouth. The blood came between his teeth in a torrent, spreading across the floor in sticky waves, and I knew that it would fill the room and drown me.

"Tetris," said Junior through the rush of blood. "Do you understand now? Do you understand, Tetris?"

"Understand what?" I shouted, standing as the sticky red tide rose, lapping at the edges of my cot. "Understand what?"

"Tetris!"

I looked down and saw that the blood had vanished. The room was dark, the bathroom still. Li sat in bed, rubbing her eye with a fist.

"What the fuck, dude?"

"Sorry," I said, lying back down. "Just a nightmare."

I curled up under the sheets, heart jackhammering

away.

"I've never heard you talk in your sleep," said Li.

"Hmm," I mumbled.

"That better not become a habit," she said. "You can't shout like that in the forest."

"Guess I'll be duct taping my mouth," I said.

"Guess so," said Li, and rolled to face the wall.

16

In the morning Cooper took us to the cafeteria for breakfast, then back to Dr. Alvarez's lab for what I presumed to be round two of Forestology 101. This time, though, he got straight to the point.

"We've got a mission for you," said Cooper.

"Course you do," said Li.

"Out in the middle of the Pacific, there are a number of volcanoes, most of them inactive, that protrude above forest level," said Cooper. "Since the sixties, we've maintained a base on one particular chain. The name of the chain is Hawaii."

"Hawaii?" I said, rolling the word over my tongue.

"Proto-Polynesian for 'Place of the Gods,'" explained Dr. Alvarez.

"Course it is," said Li.

"The reason we set up a research station there," said Cooper, "is that there's a major electromagnetic distortion a few miles off shore."

"We've been conducting experiments as discreetly as possible," said Dr. Alvarez, "but there's only so much we can learn without sending people in."

"So you want us to go," I said.

"Correct," said Cooper.

Dr. Alvarez pulled up the hologram of the alternate-Earth again. Its sapphire oceans rotated before us.

"You two simplified things tremendously when you stumbled across those artifacts. Obtaining clearance for this was going to be a nightmare. You're the obvious choice for the mission."

"What do you mean, 'you two?'" demanded Li. "What about Zip?"

Cooper grimaced. "That's where the bad news comes in."

My stomach flattened. Zip was dead, I could feel it.

"Zip's not going on any more expeditions," said Cooper, and I turned away, screwing my eyes closed.

"Motherfucker," said Li. "You let him die?"

"What?" said Cooper. "No, he's not dead. He's in the hospital and looks to be making a full recovery. But they had to take his leg off."

I remembered the foul odor that had spewed out of Zip's wound, the way the punctured skin oozed with blood and yellow pus. No more rock climbing for him, then. Although, knowing Zip, he'd figure out a way to do it with three limbs. But our trio wouldn't be setting any expedition records together, that was for sure.

"Fuck," said Li.

"Sorry," said Cooper. "But we only needed two of you anyway. The third slot goes to a scientist."

My eyelids peeled wide.

"No way," I said. "That's a suicide mission. We're not dragging dead weight out there."

"They won't be dead weight," said Cooper.

"Like hell they won't," said Li.

"The person we're sending has been training for months," said Cooper. "They might not be on the same level, but they'll know how to look out for themselves."

"Why?" I asked. "Why can't you send rangers and look at the footage afterward, like you always do?"

"We don't know what's out there," said Cooper, "and we don't know if it'll still be there when we look a second time. We might only have one shot."

"It's a suicide mission," said Li. "You want us to plunge into God knows what kind of clusterfuck, and you want us to do it with somebody we don't trust, somebody we can't possibly trust."

"Look," said Cooper, "at least give this person a chance. Let them show you what they can do. If they can't win you over, if you still want out, we can't force you to go."

"We can walk away?" asked Li. "You'll let us walk away?"

Her teeth were bared, the canines sharp.

"Of course," said Cooper. "It's a free country. Although if you agree to participate, you'll be compensated more than fairly."

Li's eyes flicked back and forth across his face. She

turned to me and twisted her mouth in a way that said *fuck it*.

"Alright," she said.

"So who's the third guy?" I said. "When do we get to meet him?"

Dr. Alvarez stirred. I'd almost forgotten about her.

"It's me," she said.

Li laughed. She leaned against the stairs, head tilted back as far as it could go, and shook with hooting laughter.

"Oh my God," she said when she'd recovered somewhat. Her cheeks were pink. "Well, I can tell you one thing, and that's that you're going to have to cut off all that beautiful hair."

"I know," said Dr. Alvarez stiffly. "I have been putting it off as long as possible."

"Oh boy," said Li. "Oh boy."

"You should take some time to think about it," said Cooper.

"No shit," said Li. "Get me out."

She headed up the stairs. I gave Dr. Alvarez a smirk and followed. After a moment Cooper came along and held the door for us.

In the hallway Li rounded on him.

"Doc better be real fucking impressive," she said.

"We'll bring you back in a couple of weeks," said Cooper, "and you can put her through whichever kinesthetic rigmarole you desire."

"I want to see Zip," I said.

"I've got a car waiting," said Cooper.

Just like that, it was over. We were free. Li and I sat in the back seat and looked out our opposite windows.

"You folks mind if I play some music?" asked our driver after a few minutes of silence.

"Whatcha got?" asked Li.

"Taj Mahal," said the driver. "Taj Mahal and the Phantom Blues Band."

"Sounds great."

So we listened to Taj Mahal and watched the highway markers whip by. It was a bright day, the sun high in the sky, no clouds in sight.

"I don't know what to say," sang Taj Mahal, "I must have had a real bad day."

During the last year of Todd's life, I'd spent countless days at the hospital, as the doctors administered chemotherapy or radiation or whatever five-percent-chance treatment they were trying that month. Nowhere was more impersonal and lifeless than a hospital. People bustled everywhere, but you were invisible to them, your misery inconsequential. Your whole life might be falling apart, but that wouldn't stop them from telling jokes and laughing as they strolled past.

We asked the lady at the information desk for Zachary Chase and she gave us his room number. Three burly men in poorly-fitted suits lounged on spindly chairs outside. They eyed us lazily as we entered.

Zip was asleep. The muscles of his face had finally relaxed, allowing his mouth to hang open. He snored quietly. His eyes, closed, were inset and dark.

"You better let him sleep," said the nurse. "It's going to be a few days before he's up to entertaining visitors."

We sat beside his bed. The EKG machine beeped.

"I'm glad he's okay," I said, because it was the only thing to say.

"Me too," said Li, looking at the place where his leg should have been propping up the blankets.

Outside in the sun, our driver leaned against the car, smoking a cigarette.

"Back already?"

"He's asleep," I said.

The driver dropped the cigarette and rubbed it out with his heel. His smile revealed a wide gap between his front teeth. It didn't look bad—just made him seem friendly.

"I can take you back to your cars, if you want," he said.

"That'd be great," said Li.

"Agent Cooper booked rooms downtown."

"Nice of him," I said.

"Mh hmm," said the driver, and opened the door.

At the hotel I dropped my bags beside the minifridge and plopped on the bed with my laptop. After finagling the complimentary internet to life, I pulled up a high-resolution satellite image of the planet.

It was the same old picture. The forest was everywhere you looked, outlining the continents, a dark, implacable green. Over the top swirled thick white clouds. On land: lighter green, yellow, brown... jungles and deserts and plains. Then the caps of the globe: brown smeared into white. Frigid wasteland. I zoomed in on the northernmost edge of the Pacific Forest. The transition was abrupt, rough-edged. The treeline fizzled out, and northward from there it was muddy and cold.

I zoomed back out and looked at the whole globe again. It was ugly.

This green-brown sphere with naked poles was diseased, syphilitic, balding. I closed one eye and recalled the world Dr. Alvarez had shown me, boundless clean water glittering blue. That was the planet I wanted. What had happened to get me stuck with this one instead?

That night, a rare thunderstorm rolled over San Diego. The windows shuddered, rain pelting against them in waves. I didn't feel like sleeping, so I watched a James Bond marathon. Around midnight I got a text from Li.

You still up?

My heart rate tripled. Did that mean what I thought it meant? This late at night, was there any other reason to send that text?

"Yeah, wanna come down the hall?" I typed, then backspaced it out.

After trying it a few different ways—"Yeah, want to hang out?" "Yeah, what's going on?"—I settled on the simplest possible reply:

Yeah

As I waited for her next message, James Bond drove a sports car out the side of a supervillain's ice fortress. Translucent shards sprayed in all directions. The car floated languorously in midair. The camera cut to a close-up of Bond's face, his cheeks smooth, no stubble, the corners of his lips hooked upward in a mischievous smile. Then the car touched down and time returned to normal.

Right when I thought I'd waited too long to reply, my phone buzzed again.

I can't sleep.

A few seconds later:

Can I come over?

I stared at the text bubble with those words in it.

Sure, room 205.

I dropped my phone and surveyed the room. Earlier, when I'd rooted through my duffel, I'd strewn clothes all over the place. Now I stuffed them back inside. My sneakers were scattered beside the door; I straightened them out.

I looked at my reflection in the bathroom mirror and couldn't help but laugh. What was I worried about? I flexed, practiced a broad grin. What did I think was going to happen? Something in my head had come unplugged. I was a teenager on his first date, trying to decide whether to put an arm around the girl during the opening credits of the movie.

When she knocked I counted to five before opening the door.

Her eyes were bright and sharp, not the least bit drowsy.

"Hey," she said, and I stood aside so she could come in.

"Raining pretty hard out there," I said, hands in my pockets.

"Sure is," she said.

For a while we watched drops come splattering out of the darkness against the wide window.

"What are you up to?" she asked, as if she couldn't tell.

"I'm watching a James Bond marathon," I said.

"Neat," she said, and sat down on the bed. After a moment I joined her.

On the screen, James Bond leaned against the bar at a classy party, exchanging sultry glances with a woman in a low-cut red dress.

"They're gonna bang," said Li.

"A bold prediction," I said.

Sure enough, James Bond followed the woman to her personal rooms. She draped herself against the doorframe and craned her neck back.

"Do you think you're enough of a man for me, Mr. Bond?" asked the woman in her huskiest voice.

"Oh, I always rise to the occasion," said James Bond.

"Thousands of years from now, archaeologists are going to discover movies like this and make all sorts of conclusions about our society," said Li.

"And they'll mostly be right," I said.

"Not everybody's a violent, sex-crazed solipsist."

"What's wrong with sex?"

She looked at me. "Nothing. I'm just saying, it's all some people think about."

"That's evolution's fault, though."

She shook her head. We watched the rest of the movie in silence. When the credits rolled, she yawned and stretched, reaching above her head.

"I actually get so bored watching TV," she said.

"Me too," I said. "I get bored most of the time, actually. Not sure what I find fun these days."

"Everything outside the forest is so beige."

I grinned. "Actually, I can think of one thing that's fun."

"Stop."

"What?"

"I hear enough of that from Zip."

"I mean, I don't kiss and tell the way he does, but my appreciation for the fairer sex is probably comparable."

"I don't doubt it."

I couldn't tell if she was giving off positive signals or not. My hands were sweaty, and my mouth was dry, but I decided to press on anyway.

"C'mon," I said, "you can't tell me you don't get the same urges."

"No comment," said Li.

"We rangers," I said, "we're good-looking guys, right? In great shape. Strong chins."

She laughed.

"Not my type," she said.

I stuck an arm out, tugged back my shirt sleeve, and flexed.

"What's not to like?"

Li looked at my bicep, then back at my face, and doubled over laughing. She shook, practically crying, and after a while she put a hand on my knee. The laughing made my heart plummet, but the hand on my knee took the sting away.

"Tetris," she said, "you're like a brother to me. I could never, ever think about you that way. I'm just not attracted to you. Sorry."

I kept my stupid grin up, although I could feel the edges drooping.

"What?" I said. "No, I mean—that's not what I was saying—I would never suggest that—"

"I'm not an idiot," she said, leaning into my shoulder. "It's sweet, actually. I'm very flattered."

I picked up the remote and flicked through the channels.

"Sorry," she said, "I just want to be up front, you know? Avoid any confusion."

"Sure," I said, punching the channel-change button. "It's fine."

"I care about you, man," she said. "We've got a good, solid friendship. Isn't that enough?"

"Of course," I said. Everything she'd said was reasonable. Why did I feel so bitter?

I put the remote down and we watched a few minutes of some Spanish-language soap opera, her cheek still leaned against my shoulder. My mind did barrel rolls five miles above. After a while, she clicked her tongue and patted my chest, then slid off the bed.

"Alright," she said. "I'm going to sleep."

"Goodnight," I said, getting up to walk her out.

"Sleep well," she said.

"You too," I said, and closed the door behind her.

Alone in the room, I paced to the window, hands behind my head. Stupid. She was bored, couldn't sleep, had wanted to come hang out. That was it. That was all it was. Why'd I have to make it into a disaster?

I tried to sleep, but between my fear of another Junior dream and my mind's determination to replay fourfold every millisecond of the evening with Li, I rolled from side to side for hours. Even the dull patter of rain couldn't lull me into unconsciousness.

Cooper met us in the hotel lobby for breakfast.

"Take a week or two off," he said, sliding an envelope across the table. "Tickets for your flight back to Seattle."

"Thanks," I said, battling a yawn.

"When Zip's doing better, we'll send him home. Maybe you can meet him at the airport."

I rubbed my exhausted eyes and made an affirmative noise.

Cooper stirred his coffee. "About the way we picked you up—"

"Don't sweat it," I said, although I could tell it was Li that Cooper was worried about. She hadn't said much, and it wasn't because she was busy eating. She'd barely touched her stack of pancakes. She had a cold glare fixed on Cooper.

"Sorry about any confusion," he said. "We really are on the same team. Just had to exercise caution, you know?"

"Understandable," I said, wanting to get out of there as soon as possible.

Cooper must have felt it too, because he took one last

gulp of coffee and pushed his chair back.

"We'll be in touch," he said, and mimed a quick salute before shrugging into his suit jacket and striding away.

"I can't stand that guy," said Li.

"I noticed," I said, "and I think he did too."

"Good."

I munched on a strawberry. My appetite was still in overdrive, and it felt amazing to sink my teeth into something firm and juicy. As I ate, I eyed Li, trying to be discreet. She hadn't said a word about the previous night, and if she didn't bring it up I had no intention of ever touching on it again.

I needed a girlfriend. That's what I needed.

We went to visit Zip before our flight, but he was asleep again, snores whistling through his nose.

"You just missed him," said the nurse. "He woke up this morning and had a snack. Poor thing's been through a lot. Going to sleep like a koala for a while."

At the airport I defeated Li in a best-of-five rock-paper-scissors match to secure myself the window seat on the plane. My strategy was to pick "rock" every time and let her overthink her own move.

"I can't believe I let you win three times with rock," she said, glowering.

I shrugged. "Some people just aren't cut out for the high-octane world of competitive rock-paper-scissors."

When I got on the plane and worked my way back to row twenty-three, there was already somebody in my seat. I scrounged in my pocket for my boarding pass. 23D. That was mine, alright. I gave its occupant another look.

It was Junior. His black eyes pulsed. The hole in his chest dribbled pus and maggots as he leaned toward me, extending a hand. When he opened his mouth, his teeth were sharpened to fine points.

My head ballooned. Dizzy, I stumbled back. Nausea came at me in wriggling waves, and I closed my eyes, focusing on keeping my breakfast down. For a moment all I could hear was a tinny ringing.

When my hearing returned, I looked again.

Junior was gone. The other passengers were staring at me. I had practically fallen into the lap of a suited man across the aisle. Muttering an apology, I hoisted myself off of him.

"What's going on?" asked Li.

Despite my wobbly legs, I managed to cram my duffel into the overhead bin.

"Nothing," I said, lowering myself into the seat. "I'm fine."

I closed my eyes, trying to slow my heart with deep, calm breaths.

You're losing your mind, said the voice in the back of my head.

I stomped it down and reached for the magazine in the seat-back pocket.

17

Our eyes concealed behind sunglasses, Li and I watched Dr. Alvarez scurry through an obstacle course. She vaulted a series of fences and climbed a net with ease. On the balance beam that followed, she looked shaky for a moment, but recovered and finished it out quickly. The next few obstacles gave her no trouble at all. To complete the course, she had to ascend a rope and ring a bell. It took her a while, but not as long as I would have expected.

"All in all," said Cooper, "an unquestionably impressive display."

Li had her arms crossed and a foot tapping furiously. She checked the stopwatch.

"Sixty-five seconds," she said, and tossed it to Cooper, who nearly dropped it. "My turn."

Dr. Alvarez came over, slick with sweat and trying not

to pant. As Li set up, the doctor cleared her throat. I became aware that she was staring at me.

"How did I do?"

In shorts and a tank top, with her hair cut short, she no longer looked like a scientist. Her chin curved up to pointy cheekbones and eyes as sharp as a diamond-tipped drill.

"Fine," I said. "Stumbled on the beam. Took too long at the end. Otherwise, fine."

"I see," said Dr. Alvarez.

Cooper indicated to Li that he was ready, and she streaked into the course. Over the fences she flew, up and over the net, along the balance beam at a sprint. The rest of the course passed in a blur. Scaling the rope took mere moments.

"Thirty-eight seconds," said Cooper when Li jogged over.

"So," said Li, "turns out sixty-five is awful."

"He said it was fine," said Dr. Alvarez, pointing at me.

Li rolled her eyes. "He's being nice because he thinks you're cute."

I made a strangled noise.

"I was being nice because I'm a nice guy," I said.

"Run it again," said Li.

Dr. Alvarez gave her a sour look. "I don't have my breath back."

"Exactly," said Li.

This time Dr. Alvarez finished in seventy-nine seconds.

"That's what I thought," said Li. "No endurance."

"This is unfair," said Dr. Alvarez, face the color of a

raspberry.

Li's glare was equal parts rage and pity. She planted a finger in Cooper's chest. "I want out. She's out of shape and her attitude's all wrong."

Cooper tried and failed to brush the hand away. "You carried a cripple through the forest for a week and a half. How is this harder than that?"

"It's not," said Li, "but that doesn't mean I want to do it."

Cooper turned to me. "What about you?"

I fiddled with my car keys. "If Li's out, I'm out."

"I thought you might say that," said Cooper. "Which is why we're prepared to offer you each ten million dollars for this expedition."

My jaw fell open.

"What?" I squawked.

"Forget it," said Li. "You can't bribe someone into suicide."

"What she means is, can we get back to you tomorrow?" I said, grabbing Li's arm.

"I thought we were going to swing by the grapple gun course," said Cooper.

"I'm sure she's a regular old expert," I said, pulling Li away. "Gotta go! Talk to you soon."

"Well, okay," said Cooper. Dr. Alvarez smoldered beside him.

In the car, Li slammed her door shut. I dropped the keys in a cup holder.

"Are you out of your mind?" she said.

"Ten million dollars, Li. Christ! Do you understand how much money that is?"

"Won't do us any good if we're dead."

"We won't die," I said. "In fact, it's safer this way, because we can retire afterward. Survive one trip and we're set for life. Otherwise we're risking our lives on expedition after expedition."

"What happened to being an explorer?" she asked. "I thought you weren't in this for the money."

I considered this and backtracked.

"It's not just about the money," I said.

"What, then?"

"You heard Cooper. This is some top-secret world-altering shit. They've got a whole electromagnetic whatchamacallit out there, just begging to be probed."

She shook her head, but I could tell that I was getting through.

"What was it you told me back in training? That the forest had to be more than what it seemed? Now we've finally got a chance to figure out the truth, and you want to chicken out?"

"I don't want to think about this right now," said Li.

"I could use a drink too."

"Not what I meant. It's four in the afternoon."

"So?"

Li sighed. "Fine."

Hamilton's Tavern had just opened an hour ago. It was deserted. At one end of the bar, a pair of businessmen dug into sloppy burgers, leaning over their plates to keep the juices from dribbling onto their clothes. At the other end of the bar sat Hollywood.

"You've got to be kidding me," said Li.

Hollywood turned at the sound of her voice.

"Ha," he barked.

"Haven't seen your ugly mug in a while," said Li, taking a seat beside him. I sat on her opposite side.

"I've been staying off the radar," said Hollywood, rubbing the bridge of his crooked nose. His drink was mostly gone.

"Any expeditions recently?"

"Nah," said Hollywood.

The bartender came by. He was a round man with eyebrows like fuzzy caterpillars.

"What can I bring you folks?"

"Recommendations?"

After enduring a long-winded spiel on the merits of various local craft breweries, I ordered something called a Speedway Stout. Li asked for a cider.

As we waited for the drinks, Li filled Hollywood in on our latest expedition. She left out the tablet and the structure in the clearing. The rest of the story was delivered in meticulous, gory detail, down to the precise velocity with which orange goo exited the abdomen of a spider upon forced implosion via gigantic ape fists.

"Anyway," said Li when she'd finished, after we sat in silence for a minute or two, "How have you been?"

"Truth is," said Hollywood, scratching his chin, "I've been kind of fucked up."

"What?"

Hollywood's eyes flicked over Li's face, then mine, as he dug at the dirt under his fingernails.

"Forget it," he said, and finished his drink.

The skin of my arms pebbled up.

"You can't say something like that and then say it's nothing," said Li.

"I'm fine," said Hollywood.

"Bad dreams?" I suggested.

Hollywood tilted his head. His fingers ceased their fidgeting.

"No dreams," said Hollywood pleasantly. "Have you been having dreams, Tetris?"

It spilled out before I could stop it. "Dreams about Junior. Except his eyes are black and he's got a hole in his chest."

"Sucks," said Hollywood, with a sarcastic whistle. "PTSD, maybe?"

I grimaced. If I was actually going crazy, the last thing I wanted was for Hollywood to know.

"Is that what happened the other night?" asked Li, scrunching her eyebrows. "When you jumped out of bed screaming?"

Hollywood chuckled. "Some things never change."

"Fuck off," said Li.

"When's the wedding? Dibs on best man."

"You can be a bridesmaid," I offered.

"If I ever get married, I'm not inviting either of you," said Li.

"Ouch," said Hollywood.

When Li turned away, Hollywood's eyes flitted across her body. Suddenly I was furious. What right did he have to ogle her in public?

He caught me staring and grinned. His canines were yellow.

"Hollywood," said Li.

"What?"

"How much would they have to pay you to take a random civilian on an expedition?"

"A little extra, I guess. Ten thousand bucks?"

"It wouldn't worry you that you couldn't trust her?"

"You think I trust rangers?"

I made a mental note that this was the most stereotypically "Hollywood" thing I had ever heard.

"Look," said Hollywood, leaning on the bar, "every time we go out there, it's with the understanding that nobody, however experienced, is immune to the occasional fuck-up. Zip fucked up, didn't he? And he was an acceptably competent little munchkin."

"The chances would be so much higher."

"That doesn't matter if you respond to fuck-ups intelligently."

"You mean you'd let them die," I said.

"Hell yeah," said Hollywood. "I admire what you did for Zip, but you have to admit it was stupid."

"We knew we could save him," said Li.

"I counted six or seven places where you should have been dead," said Hollywood.

"But we're alive."

"Point is, you got lucky," said Hollywood.

I replayed the scene in the forest, replacing Zip with Dr. Alvarez. Would we have descended into the pit for her?

"I can't believe you'd take someone along only to abandon them," said Li. "That's disgusting."

"Come on," said Hollywood. "Long before we left, I'd tell them: look. If you fuck up, I'm not risking my life to save you. You'll just fucking die."

Which must have resonated with Li, because in the morning she greeted Dr. Alvarez and Cooper with open arms.

"Doc," said Li, "you can come along."

Dr. Alvarez smiled. "Thanks for giving me a chance."

"I'm not finished. You can come along, but you have to understand one thing: I'm not risking my life to save you."

"Reasonable."

"If you fuck up, I'm leaving you to die. Understood?"

The smile wavered a bit. "Understood."

"I mean, we're not going to actively try to get you killed or anything," I offered.

"Don't let him take the edge off of it," said Li. "I don't give you good odds. This is fifty-fifty, at best."

"Okay," said Dr. Alvarez.

"Are you okay with that? Are you okay with a fifty percent chance that this mission kills you? Is it that important to you?"

Dr. Alvarez looked at Cooper. He shrugged.

"Yes," said Dr. Alvarez.

Li squinted at the clouds sailing across the sky. Dopplered strains of a passing car's music overlaid the sound of distant crows interfacing.

"Alright," she said. "When do we start your training?"

"Whoa," said Cooper. "What do you mean, 'start?'"

"She needs two months, at least," said Li. "Put her in with Rivers' next batch."

"She's already had months of perfectly intensive training," said Cooper.

I got up in his face. "Sell her short on this and it'll be your fault when she dies."

"I'll do the training," said Dr. Alvarez.

Then she smiled at me, and something inside me melted, and I realized maybe I did think she was cute after all.

18

My answering machine was blinking when I arrived in my apartment. I hit play and untied my shoes.

"Hey, it's your dad."

I almost slammed the delete button, but stopped with my finger hovering above it.

"Just wanted to check in and see how things were going. Call me back if you want. Miss you."

Then a few seconds of silence before the click that signified his hanging up. I put my shoes back on and went to visit Zip.

When I rang the bell he came over on his crutches and yanked the door open.

"Welcome, welcome," he shouted, beaming.

Chomper the pug ran tight ovals around us, emitting breathless little barks. I rubbed him behind the ears.

"Would you look at that," I said. "He didn't even pee himself."

"Don't jinx it," said Zip. "Hurry up. I'm watching a

documentary about Magellan."

I followed him to the living room. There was a hint of impatience, but otherwise he seemed to have the hang of the crutches.

"Who's Magellan?"

"You really didn't learn a thing in school, huh?"

"Dead Italian people were never a top priority."

"Ferdinand Magellan was one of the greatest explorers in history," said Zip. "Dude flew an airship around the world back in the 1500s."

"Oh. That guy."

"And he was Portuguese, not Italian."

"Of course. What'd they give him?"

"Hmm?"

"For finishing that trip? Did they make him a knight? Did the Portuguese have knights?"

"Oh, Magellan himself didn't make it."

"I thought you said—"

"No, his crew finished the journey without him. Somewhere off the coast of Southeast Asia, Ferdy got cocky and floated too close to the canopy. Pterodactyl snatched him right off the deck."

"No shit."

Chomper had his tongue out. He mostly sat on the couch next to Zip, but every once in a while he hopped down and ran over to me for a pat on the head.

We watched the documentary for a while, but I could tell that Zip was no longer interested. He kept reaching for his phone to check the time.

"Okay," I said, "you've obviously got questions."

He flicked the TV off and tossed the remote aside. "One moment you're dragging me through the forest. Then I wake up in a hospital bed."

"They didn't tell you anything?"

"I mean," said Zip, "this sleazeball came to visit a couple times. Dressed like Frank Sinatra but without the handsome."

"What'd he say?"

"*You're not in trouble. Your friends are fine.*' Bullshit like that."

"Anything else?"

"Said if I kept my mouth shut about the tablet they'd set me up with a fat pension."

"Must have been Cooper," I said. "Smiled like a snake?"

"Yeah."

"Me and Li have seen a lot of him."

I could tell he felt left out, so I filled the silence with the first thing that popped into my head.

"The forest's not supposed to be there," I said. "It's supposed to be water."

"What?"

"Like, instead of forest—everything that's forest, is supposed to be water."

"That's two thirds of the globe."

"I know," I said. "They showed us what it would look like."

"Are you allowed to be telling me this?"

"Fuck them," I said, electrified. "I'm telling you. I don't

care what they think."

His shoulders relaxed. "What do you mean, 'supposed to be?'"

"Millions of years ago, we went from having water to having forests. And they think it has something to do with the tablets."

Zip rapped his knuckles against his leg. "Why did they tell you that? Why not just tell you to shut up, the way they did with me?"

I watched his face carefully. "They want us to go on an expedition."

He snorted. "Right."

"Me and Li and a scientist. We're supposed to investigate a magnetic disturbance. Or something. I'm not totally clear on that part."

Zip rubbed his eyes and rested his face on his palms. All I could see was the taut line of his mouth.

"You alright?"

He took a moment to respond. "I'm so pissed, man. That should be me out there, but I fucked up, and I'm going to have to live with that the rest of my life."

"At least you're alive," I said.

"I kinda wish I'd died," said Zip. He scratched Chomper behind the ears. "I don't mean that."

"You better not," I said, trying to think of what Li would say.

Get over yourself, fuckface. I went through hell to save you. Where's my thank-you card?

"What am I going to do, Tetris? I mean, what am I

going to do with my life?"

"What does anybody do? Find a job. Find a girl. Chill out and enjoy yourself."

"Right," said Zip, but he didn't sound convinced.

"Look," I said, "we're hitting Thai Restaurant for dinner. Want us to pick you up?"

I was pleased to see him brighten at the thought.

"Thank God," he said. "I mean, my sister's great. She's been going light years out of her way to take care of me. But... let's just say she's not going to be winning a cooking show any time soon."

When Li and I picked him up, he'd put on a nice shirt and rolled up his empty pant leg, fastening it with safety pins. At the restaurant he even managed to grin when the waitress, who'd seen us often enough to notice the missing leg, asked what happened. After regaling her with the tale—in this version, the culprit was a Tyrannosaurus Rex, and the story did not end well for the reptile in question— Zip even managed to requisition her phone number, scribbled upon a napkin, which he carefully folded and placed in his pocket.

And for once, instead of making a snarky comment, Li gave Zip a congratulatory smack on the back, and then we were all laughing, and for the first time in a long while I knew that everything was going to be okay.

19

The dreams were getting worse. They came in low and hot over the trees and through my bedroom window at night. In the mornings a shadow of myself was sweated into the sheets, leaving a faint, salty silhouette even when the fabric dried. I started switching them out twice a week.

One day at the grocery store, hand-length centipedes writhed among the oranges. I had to step around a pool of blood beside a yellow "Wet Floor" sign in Aisle Six. I ignored the hallucinations and went to check out. At first the cashier seemed normal enough, but when she turned to grab my receipt, her cheek had a ragged hole. Clean white teeth showed through like rows of gum pellets.

I never called my dad back, but I didn't delete his voicemail, either.

The night before the flight to Hawaii, I sat in bed watching shapes glide across the walls. Sometimes I could tell that they were shadows, chased by headlights passing on the street. Other times they were driven by no light source I could detect. If I stared straight at them, the shapes froze, pretending to be natural. It was only out of the corner of my eye that I could catch them moving.

According to policy, rangers were supposed to report for psychological evaluation at the first sign of mental instability. I had a feeling I was way past that point, but there was no way I was turning myself in. Not now, one expedition away from ten million dollars. I could buy an awful lot of top-notch psychiatric care with ten million dollars. I wanted the money so bad that I'd started to come up with worst-case scenarios, to prepare for the potential disappointment. Maybe Cooper would turn out to be a lying sack of shit. Maybe Congress would cut funding for whatever agency Cooper belonged to. Maybe nuclear war would break out. But mostly I constructed lists of all the things I'd buy when the check came through. A midnight-silver electric sports car. A lifelong subscription to every magazine in America. Even when I totaled up everything I could imagine, it didn't come close to denting ten million dollars.

I wanted to tell Li. I wanted to come clean and tell her about the time I saw Junior on the plane, about the centipedes and the cashier's cheek-hole and the insomnia and the night sweats and everything. But as hard as it had been to convince her to come along, I couldn't give her any excuse to back out.

And yet...

I had a sneaking suspicion that I was putting her life in danger. That I was going to get all three of us killed. Because the psychological instability rules existed for a reason, and the reason was that crazy people tended to last approximately as long as a strawberry Popsicle in the forest.

But this was ten million dollars we were talking about. So when I lugged my duffel onto the plane and plopped into the seat beside Li, and she asked what was wrong with my eyes, I told her not to worry about it.

Soon we were soaring over the Pacific and I was slumped against the window catching up on sleep.

Hours later I woke to find Li deep in the thickest book I'd ever seen.

"What's that?" I asked.

She licked a finger and turned the page. "What were you doing instead of sleeping last night?"

"Watching Seinfeld reruns. That a crime?"

Li slowly shook her head. "It's *Infinite Jest*."

"What?"

"The book, dumbass."

I looked at it. It was twice as thick as the Bible.

"What's it about?"

"Tennis."

"That whole thing's about tennis?"

"There's other stuff, too."

"I didn't know you liked to read."

"Nothing else to do."

I smacked my lips and swallowed, trying to clear the sour crust of saliva from the roof of my mouth.

"How long was I out?"

Li checked her watch. "Five hours."

I sidled past her to stretch my legs in the aisle. We were the only passengers except for a few people I didn't recognize up in the front. The empty seats creeped me out. I was used to planes that buzzed with tangled conversation and the rustling of magazines. Except for the thrum of the engines, this plane was silent.

I noticed Sergeant Rivers a few rows behind us. His single eye was focused downward, perhaps at a book of his own.

"Hey," I said, "I didn't know Rivers was coming."

Li tapped her bookmark against the page and raised an eyebrow.

"Rivers," I said, and went to point. Then I saw that his face was sloughing off, sliding into his lap, the eye-holes and mouth elongating like putty as the skin pulled loose from his red-slicked skull, and I had to grab a seat and close my eyes to stop the flood of nausea.

When it passed, I straightened and tried to pretend that nothing had happened. Li gave me a positively eviscerating glare.

"Alright," she said, "I've had enough. What is wrong with you today?"

"Stupid joke," I grunted. I was having a hard time concentrating over the ringing in my right ear. I fought the urge to stick a finger in there and silence it.

"You were making a joke? And then you keeled over, I assume because of how awful your joke was?"

I tried to smile and managed at least to bare my teeth.

"Airsick," I offered. I forced myself to glance back at

the place where I'd seen Rivers. The seat was as empty as the rest of the plane.

I wondered what I'd see next. A headless Zip hang-gliding across the sky? Hollywood swinging like Tarzan through the forest?

"I don't understand why you're lying," said Li.

"I tried to make a joke and got airsick right at the punchline. Arrest me."

"Fine. Don't tell me. Jeez."

I felt guilty, but the guilt was nothing compared to the relief of escaping detection. Wiping sweat from my forehead—why was I sweating? The cabin was freezing—I went to the back of the plane to relieve myself. I stayed in the bathroom a long time, staring into the vibrating mirror.

When we stepped onto the sprawling black runway in Hawaii, Dr. Alvarez and Cooper were waiting for us.

"Welcome to paradise," said Cooper.

Tropical trees, draped with vines and moss, encircled the airstrip. In the distance, guard towers rose above the jungle. Beyond that reared the spine of a green-black mountain, curving away to the south.

It was hot on the tarmac. I shouldered the duffel, waiting for them to lead the way, but Cooper stayed put.

"How was the flight?" he asked.

"It was fine," said Li.

"Yes," I said briskly. "It was fine."

Dr. Alvarez squeezed her lips in a way that said I don't believe you, but I am not about to pry. Cooper seemed oblivious.

"Great! Come on, I'll give you '*El Grande Tourino*,' as they say!"

He took us to a dull gray Jeep, babbling all the while. As we drove, Dr. Alvarez delivered another unprompted lecture.

"It's likely that islands like these would have been tourist hotspots in a world with oceans," she said. "The edges would be covered in sand. Like a lake shore, but much finer and softer material, eroded by the water and deposited on the coast over millions of years."

I watched the foliage zip by. Every once in a while there was a burst of color as a tropical bird, startled by our passage, took flight.

"What would it look like?" I asked. "All that water?"

"There would be waves," said Dr. Alvarez. "You've probably seen waves on lakes. But ocean waves would be different. Much more powerful. When they hit the shore, the tallest ones would crest, curling up and tumbling down."

I'd imagined a flat plain of water, still and placid and boundless. The way Dr. Alvarez described it, oceans sounded as violent and chaotic as the forest.

The military base was encircled by a seventy-foot buffer of bare dirt. The trees were gone, but no one had bothered to clear the stumps, which dotted the no-man's-land like pimples. As we pulled through a gate into the complex, we passed scaffolding that bridged a gaping hole in the wall. A crane worked to clear debris.

"What happened there?" asked Li.

"Oh, we had a little incident," said Cooper. "Nothing to worry about."

"Whatever it was took a big chunk out of your base," said Li. Piles of rubble indicated places where buildings close to the wall had been flattened.

"Nothing duct tape and elbow grease can't fix."

I tried to guess at the size of the creature in question. "Subway snake?"

"Bingo," said Cooper. "Have no fear. The beast was brought low by good old-fashioned American grit and ingenuity."

"Sure," said Li, eying the high-caliber weaponry mounted on the parapet.

"I'll admit: the forest doesn't want us here," said Cooper. "It keeps sending eviction notices, but we are some persistent squatters indeed."

His voice oozed confidence, but his Adam's apple bobbed when he glanced at the wall. I had a feeling he couldn't wait to head back to the mainland. His fear soothed my nerves. I might be losing my mind, but at least I wasn't a coward.

"How far is the shore?" I asked.

"Five miles," said Dr. Alvarez.

Li wiped sweat off the tip of her nose. "You've got subway snakes coming five miles up the coast to screw with you?"

Cooper tried to fix his tie. The hot, soggy air had rendered the fabric hopelessly flaccid. I would have bet serious money that his suit jacket concealed sweat stains the size of Rhode Island.

"Guess we do," he said. "Maybe you can help us figure out why."

20

Li and I didn't talk much that night, even when Cooper took us to the room where we'd be staying and finally left us alone. She could tell that I was keeping something from her, and she didn't like it. I couldn't blame her. I'd own up to everything the instant the expedition was over.

In the room we'd been assigned, the bedspreads were generous, patterned inexplicably with palm trees and setting orange suns. The floor was scuffed. The light switches were canted. Three vaguely impressionist landscape paintings were bolted onto the walls. The overall effect was of a bad hotel pretending to be a mediocre hotel. I fell asleep immediately.

Soon I dreamed I woke up in the room with Li. Everything seemed normal—she was in her bed, fast asleep, and so far blood wasn't seeping out of cracks in the walls or anything—but I could tell it was a dream. I felt no fear, just dull expectation. Maybe I was getting used to the nightmares. The terror was gone, replaced by cool

151

acceptance of whatever fucked-up vision I was about to face.

Something pulled me to the window. I surveyed the dark arteries of the base. In the distance, searchlights from guard towers played back and forth, scanning the stump-ridden no-man's-land. The beams of light spat fleeting yellow polygons across the ramparts.

The realness of these dreams continued to amaze me. When I pinched my arm and twisted, I felt the sting. I closed my eyes and listened. The only sound was Li's breathing, taking in air and then, after a long silence, letting it out softly. She breathed like she was rationing oxygen, holding onto each lungful until it became pure carbon dioxide.

Gradually, I became aware of another sound, a soft plopping like clumps of peat falling out of a wheelbarrow.

Plop. Plop.

It came from outside the window. Reluctantly, I opened my eyes and looked.

In the center of the street, clumps popped up and away from a growing mound. I fixed my eyes on the bulge, ready to witness the birth of whatever lay beneath.

Slowly, patiently, a black dome emerged. Long antennae frisked the air. Satisfied with the taste, the dome revealed itself to be the head of an enormous centipede. Out into the open it wriggled, hairy with a million terrible legs, freeing itself from the ragged wound in the earth.

More centipedes followed the first, side-winding out of the hole and dispersing in all directions. So far, this was one of the tamer dreams. There was something cathartic about watching them emerge. Something about the way they shed their cloaks of dirt.

"Tetris?" said Li.

I smiled. "This is the part where I look and you've got eight eyes, or your arms have been torn off, right?"

"What?"

I turned to look. Dream-Li was sitting up in bed, rubbing the corners of her eyes. Her body parts appeared to be intact.

"What's going on, Tetris?"

"This is a dream," I said, and snickered.

"This is not a dream, Tetris," said Li.

"Ha! Arguing with a dream," I said. "Guess I really am losing my mind."

"You dumb—what the fuck is *Tetris get out of the way!*"

Something thunked against the window. I spun to see a centipede pressed against the glass. It reared back, a hundred legs writhing in the air, then slammed against the window again.

The glass spiderwebbed. I fell out of the chair, kicking my legs like propellers, suddenly very, very afraid.

"Okay," I said, "not a dream."

"Not a dream not a dream not a dream," agreed Li. "Where's my gun?"

They hadn't given us weapons yet. I scrambled to the corner and tugged on my jeans. Li dressed in equally frenzied fashion while the centipede explored the cracks in the glass with its complicated mouthparts.

"Guns," said Li. "We need guns. Big ones."

The centipede rammed its head through the glass and came slithering in.

We flung the door shut behind us and ran down the hall, pounding on the walls.

"Wake up," I shouted. "Wake up! Wake up!"

A distant alarm began to wail. The centipede exploded through the closed door and slammed against the opposite wall before steadying itself and hurtling after us.

"Down the stairs," said Li.

"You want to go down there?"

"You want to get trapped on the roof?"

We took the stairs three at a time. Outside, chaos reigned. Floodlights reflected off the carapaces that glided everywhere. A Jeep careened past, dragging a centipede that fought to wriggle aboard. The centipede scream-hissed as a barrage of point-blank shots tore its face to bits. When the bullets reached its brain, the unwanted passenger let go all at once, spasming in the street. Freed of the weight, the Jeep veered left. The driver had scarcely regained control when he ran right over another centipede and the whole vehicle vaulted into the air. Dimly, I noted the arc of the fluids that splooshed out of the creature where the tires had made contact, the orange and green mural those fluids left on the wall of the building adjacent.

Then the Jeep face-planted into a wall, and whatever munitions it had been carrying went up with a roar. For a moment a sun bloomed, the floodlights dim in comparison, and then Li was tugging me in the opposite direction as bits of Jeep and God-knows-what-else rained down around us.

We came across the desecrated body of a soldier—it was his top half; a smeared trail of blood led into an alley, where his lower half was presumably being devoured—and Li snagged the rifle out of his stiff fingers. She checked the magazine as we ran.

"Mag's full," she called.

Gunfire. I looked up just in time to see a centipede lunge at a soldier standing on the roof. It tackled him into space, his weapon spraying into the sky, and somersaulted over us. The centipede hit the pavement upside down with a crunch. As the creature writhed, Li stepped up, jammed the barrel against its chin, and pulled the trigger.

Miraculously, the soldier seemed to have survived. I vaulted the centipede's death throes and skidded to his side.

"Where's Cooper?" I asked, helping him to his feet.

"Who?" he choked, blood dribbling out of his mouth. His legs hung limp.

"Can you stand? Hello?"

The soldier's eyes rolled back.

"His back's broken, Tetris," said Li. "Leave him."

I wiped blood off his face. The soldier was my age or younger, his cheeks smooth, with a shadow of stubble along his chin. I swung him across my shoulders.

"Oh, God, Tetris," said Li. "You can't move someone whose back is broken."

"We can't leave him here," I said. "Go."

She went, and I followed. We ran, and in the distance somebody's flamethrower lit up the night, a blossoming orange flower, and we kept on running.

21

We found Dr. Alvarez in the turret of an armored vehicle near the center of the base. She grinned bright enough to light up the courtyard when she saw us.

"Evening," she said. Around us, burly soldiers manned improvised barricades. They hardly seemed to notice our presence, so intently did they peer into the gelatinous darkness.

"Where's Cooper?" asked Li.

"Down below," said Dr. Alvarez, clapping a gloved hand on the armored roof.

"I knew we'd find him cowering," said Li.

"Not cowering," shouted Cooper, his voice bouncing, muffled and irate, out of the depths of the vehicle. "Someone has to stay back and dispense strategic guidance to our boots on the ground."

"Positively Patton-esque of you," said Dr. Alvarez, giving me a wink I couldn't help but feel was a bit flirtatious. I shifted the unconscious soldier to a better position across my shoulders.

"We need a medic," I said.

Dr. Alvarez pointed to a nearby tent.

"Incoming," shouted someone.

Dr. Alvarez took hold of the machine gun and hammered away. Her whole body jittered with the recoil.

"Jesus," muttered Li, tugging my arm. "She's not what I expected, I'll give her that."

The doctor's lips pulled back from her teeth in a gleeful predatory sneer. As we headed toward the medical tent, I thought I heard her laughing, although it was hard to tell over the fusillade.

"I think I like her," I said, looking for a place to lay the injured soldier down.

"I know," said Li.

"Not like that."

As a medic rushed over, Li gave me a look that said: *Yes, like that.*

"Okay, maybe," I admitted, trying to lower my human cargo as gingerly as possible onto the gurney.

"If it gets you to stop pining after me, I guess I can't complain."

The way she said it pissed me off. What kind of friend would taunt you about something like that?

"Was he bit?" snapped the medic.

"I don't know," I said. "Maybe? One of them tackled him off a rooftop."

The medic had wide, round eyes, like a baby's, and his

helmet was a couple sizes too large. The effect was more Pee Wee Herman than grizzled battlefield doctor. He bent over the injured soldier, checking his pulse.

If it gets you to stop pining after me. Christ. She probably derived some sick satisfaction out of rubbing it in. As if the initial rejection didn't hurt enough.

"He's dead," said the medic, waving an orderly over.

I stared at him. All the shit about my crush on Li sure seemed insignificant now. There was an intolerable silent ringing inside my chest. "What?"

"Get out of the way, buddy. He's gone."

The orderly wheeled the stretcher away. I thought about how close I'd been to the centipede in our room, the horrible face pressed against the window. Not the closest I'd been to death. Still—very close. That glass couldn't have been more than a quarter-inch thick.

As a kid I'd been fascinated by multi-legged creatures. Fat spiders perched atop webs in every corner of my garage. The biggest ones lived up in the crevices where the garage door slid into the ceiling. Those only came out at night. Sometimes I'd go out with a flashlight to have a look. They were big enough that I could see them looking back at me. The shiny eyes never blinked, no matter how long we stared at each other.

Sometimes I made it my mission to exterminate them. Sprayed them off their webs with insecticide, watched them crumple up and ricochet off the concrete. Spiders shrank four or fivefold when they died. Shriveled up like they were trying to hide. They never made a sound. Or maybe they made the same sounds that forest spiders did, and their voices were too quiet to hear.

No matter how many I killed, the spiders always came back.

Once, when I was twelve, my dad put his foot in an old sneaker and a brown recluse bit him on the ankle. I was there in the basement when it happened. He swore and slapped at the spider, over and over, pulverizing it with the heel of his hand.

When the brown recluse had been reduced to a leggy smear half on his ankle and half on his palm, my dad took the sneakers upstairs and put them in a garbage bag, then tied it off and dumped it in the trash bin outside. Didn't say a word the whole time. A few hours later, a vivid red bulls-eye mark had formed on his ankle; he went to the urgent care clinic down the street. I stayed home and scoured the basement with a flashlight and my trusty can of insecticide, knocking over promising hidey-holes.

Someone in the med tent screamed and screamed. I couldn't think of anything to say to Li, so I walked away.

The night had assumed a ringing silence. In the distance, a few tongues of flame still tickled the sky. The worst of the assault seemed to have passed.

Cooper must have felt it too, because he'd ventured into the open. He stood beside Dr. Alvarez, scraping at grease spots on his plaid pajama sleeves.

"Nice PJs," said Li.

"Yes, well," said Cooper, his frown intensifying, "I didn't have time to don the proper accoutrements."

"Accoutrements," whooped Dr. Alvarez, her cheeks flushed.

"You alright there, Doc?" asked Li.

Dr. Alvarez clapped a hand on Li's shoulder. "I have never felt better in twenty-eight years."

"We'll see how you're doing once the adrenaline wears off," I said.

The next morning, Dr. Alvarez could barely keep her nose out of her oatmeal.

"Sorry for all the trouble last night," said Cooper as he peeled a banana. His suit was a notch or two more disheveled than usual.

"We still heading into the forest today?" asked Li, an eyebrow arched in Dr. Alvarez's direction.

"Perhaps not," said Cooper. "We'll take the afternoon off and get you a good night's sleep."

"How do you know the same thing won't happen again tonight?" I asked.

"If something like that happened every night, there wouldn't be a base here," said Cooper.

My sausage patty had grown several tiny human eyes. I pushed my tray away.

"Not hungry?" asked Li.

"Lost my appetite," I said. The ringing had returned. Please, I thought, not now.

I rubbed my eyes, and when I opened them again, the sausage patty was its normal eyeless self. Even the ringing had receded somewhat. Which felt like a good sign. Maybe I could control it? I made a mental note to confront the next vision head-on, to try and will it out of existence.

"You were a bundle of laughs last night, Doc," said Li.

"Humpf," said Dr. Alvarez, yawning into the back of her hand.

"Can tell a lot about somebody by the way they act when their life's in danger," said Li, smirking at Cooper.

Cooper cleared his throat and squinted across the room, pushing omelette around his plate.

That afternoon, the three of us—Li, Dr. Alvarez, and me—sat on the roof in lawn chairs and watched the breeze rustle the jungle. Nobody said much. Li read her gigantic book, which she'd salvaged from our room, licking a finger each time she turned a page. I closed my eyes behind dark glasses and savored the warmth of the sun. Soon we'd be back in perpetual dusk.

"What's the worst thing out there?"

I ignored the question, partly because the heat had lulled me to the brink of sleep, and partly because I wasn't entirely sure the words had come from Dr. Alvarez and not my own tormented subconscious. Li closed her book, the reams of pages meeting with a thunk.

"You learned all about the forest," said Li. "Don't you have your own opinion? Flesh wasps? Lots of people pick the flesh wasps."

"Well, I didn't learn everything," said Dr. Alvarez. "Anyway it's different in the classroom. You've been out there. What are you most scared of?"

I wondered if they thought I was asleep.

"None of the monsters keep me up at night," said Li,

"because when you think about it there's nothing evil in them. Just a bunch of animals trying to survive."

"So—nothing scares you?"

"That's not what I said."

"Sounded like it to me."

"I mean, sure, some deaths seem more unpleasant than others, and I want to avoid them. Like getting drained out by a mosquito. Doesn't sound fun. All the fluid in your body sucked out just like that—*bloop*. But as long as I use my brain, it's never going to happen. I'm smarter than the forest. I'm smarter than the mosquitoes and wasps and lizards and snakes. So the only thing that scares me is the chance I might fuck up."

A breeze passed over, carrying a sweet, leafy smell. When I listened closely I could hear Dr. Alvarez breathing in the chair beside me. I wondered what it would be like to kiss her. Somehow I imagined her lips as softer than the average set of lips. My own lips were chapped, scraped raw. I had an awful habit of biting them, tearing away at loose skin, especially when I was stressed, which these days was most of the time.

Maybe after this expedition I could retire to a villa somewhere with Dr. Alvarez and snog her fluffy soft lips day in and day out. No stress. We could grill steaks in the back yard and toss tennis balls to a cadre of adorable huskies. The word "snog" was just perfect for what I wanted to do to Dr. Alvarez's lips.

"Actually, there's one thing that does scare me," said Li.

"Hmm?"

"That fucking tablet," said Li. "Because whatever made that tablet—it isn't dumb. It might even be smarter than me. It's smart, and for all we know it's evil too. And that's the scariest fucking thing I can imagine."

22

As we delved into the forest, it became increasingly obvious that Dr. Alvarez operated as a sort of parachute slowing the expedition's forward momentum. She insisted on stopping every fifteen yards to pluck samples of vegetation or animal dung with a pair of steel pincers that hung at her hip.

"Honestly, Doc," said Li on the second day, "I understand that you came out here to perpetrate some serious science, and as far as I'm concerned, more power to you. But if we keep on at our current ratio of science to walking, we're never going to get anywhere."

"Yes, of course," said Dr. Alvarez, prodding with the tip of her pincers at a bulging yellow plant bulb. "It's all so fascinating, you know?"

"I'd be careful with that," I said, pointing at the bulb. "You're not going to like the smell that comes out if you pop it."

Dr. Alvarez gave me a wide-eyed look of impending guilt, steel pincers frozen mid-prod.

"Oh, no," I said. "Don't even think about it."

"But you can't just say something like that and expect me to leave it alone," said Dr. Alvarez. "Now I have to pop it. You know that. It's basic human nature."

"Oh, Christ," said Li, "at least let us get to the other side of the clearing first."

Something big rustled through a thick stand of razorgrass.

"Up!" hissed Li, and the three of us readied our grapple guns.

I aimed and fired in one fluid motion. Hook secured, I zipped upward, a few milliseconds behind Li. Then Dr. Alvarez's bolt, fired a bit late and well off the mark, careened against the trunk and rebounded into emptiness. As it flew, trailing its impossibly thin cord, the missed hook generated a horrible silence.

"She missed," I said, hanging upside-down with my feet braced against the branch. Before Li could respond, I dove into space, cord whizzing out of my grapple gun as I fell toward the doctor, who stood, dumbstruck, facing the quick-rippling wall of razorgrass—

Out into the open stampeded a towering avian creature, dubbed the "Megadodo" by rangers, a blunt-beaked, dim-eyed, fat-bodied bird with splayed pebbly talons and tufts of down jutting every which way. Confronted by Dr. Alvarez, with another human plummeting from the sky and a third not far behind, the Megadodo squawked and fled, stubby wings flapping.

"Oh my God," said Dr. Alvarez, a palm pressed against

her cheek.

"I thought you knew your way around a grapple gun?" said Li, dropping to the ground with the thoughtless grace of a gymnast.

"I do, I just—"

"You should be dead. Actually I'm mad that you aren't dead. Because that is the saddest, most mind-blowingly imbecilic first-week-rookie fuck-up I have ever seen."

"I'm sorry, Li, I just—"

"I can't believe it! I knew this was going to happen. Tetris, did I not say that this was going to happen?"

I retracted my grapple gun's line. Thank God it had been a Megadodo and not a snake or a scorpion. Watching another decent person get impaled by a stinger seemed like exactly the kind of thing that would push me over the edge into prescription-strength insanity.

"Ninety-nine-point-nine percent of things that produce that kind of noise in razorgrass are class-one badass motherfucking forest things you *do not want to fuck with*," said Li, very conspicuously *not* shouting. "You are the luckiest person I have ever met, Doc, you know that? You miss your fucking grapple and don't even run, just stand there like a cow in a slaughterhouse, slack-jawed, mooing, and the thing that comes out of the bushes is a motherfucking MEGADODO?"

Dr. Alvarez, to her credit, met Li's gaze.

"I'm sorry," she said, "but I do know how to use the grapple gun. It must have been nerves. I haven't missed a shot like that in months."

"We're turning around," said Li. "I thought I could watch you die, Doc. I really did. But when you missed that grapple, a thirty-wheeler hit me full in the chest."

"We can still do it," said Dr. Alvarez. "I'll be careful, okay? I won't rush it next time."

I squatted in a footprint left by the Megadodo. When I lifted my head, a fourth person had appeared in the clearing. It was Junior, legs crossed as he leaned against a trunk. He grinned at me over Li and Dr. Alvarez. The scorpion was nowhere to be seen, although the hole in Junior's chest remained, crawling with flies.

I'd almost forgotten how tall he was. I stared him right in his featureless eyes, willing him to disappear.

He kept smiling.

"You're not real," I muttered. "You're a hallucination. Go."

Junior's smile broadened. A red worm poked out of his ear.

I closed my eyes and counted to five. When I opened them, instead of vanishing, Junior strolled toward me, pulling the worm out of his ear hand over hand. It just kept coming. He passed between Dr. Alvarez and Li and dropped three feet of worm, coiled and wriggling, at my feet.

"Not real?" he said, smile morphing to a sneer. "Why don't you listen? Why don't you listen why don't you listen WHY DON'T YOU LISTEN LISTEN LISTEN—"

"Go!" I shouted, as his words reverberated in my skull, leaving divots and keening pain. With a sarcastic leer,

Junior vanished.

I felt the ground where he'd stood, temples pounding. Li and Dr. Alvarez stared at me.

"Excuse me?" said Li.

"Go on. With the mission, I mean," I said, dusting my hands on my pants. "Doc fucked up. It was a wake-up call, sure. But she'll be more careful from now on."

Dr. Alvarez beamed at me in a way that would normally have left my entire body tingling. At the moment all I could muster was an upward contortion of my lips.

She didn't ask to stop even once the rest of the afternoon, and most of the next morning, although I caught her staring wistfully at just about every discarded arthropod exoskeleton, cluster of flowers, and pyramid of excrement we passed.

The next few days passed quickly. Though the forest screeched and trilled, its inhabitants left us alone. Part of this was due to Li's grim, silent concentration as she led the way, SCAR at the ready. At the slightest rustle of undergrowth, she would raise a hand to stop us, and we'd stand listening, holding our breath, until Li decided it was safe to proceed.

At night, I was tortured by nightmares. I lost track of the ways I saw Dr. Alvarez, Zip and Li murdered in these dreams: disemboweled, swallowed whole, set aflame by fire ants. Mercifully, I never cried out or attempted to wriggle out of my sleeping bag. I merely woke, again and again, repeating words of reassurance to myself as sweat pooled in the inlets of the bag's acrylic interior.

On the fifth day we came across an antlion pit and paused to drink out of our canteens.

"Stay away from that," said Li, pointing at the pit. It was longer than it was wide, a dirt-sloped trench, the bottom out of sight unless you approached the edge.

"What's in there?" asked Dr. Alvarez.

"Mobile home-sized bug with totally wacko pincers," I said, miming with the thumb and index finger of my left hand.

"Ah," said Dr. Alvarez, "Myrmeleon Maximus. Colloquially, an antlion."

"Yeah," I said. "That."

"I wish I could get a look," she said.

"No you don't," I said.

The forest moves at several speeds. At the low end, there's the imperceptible rate at which the trees grow, elbowing one another out of the way as they scramble for sunlight. Then the speed with which creeper vines extend, measurable on a daily if not hourly basis. The gradual creep that a tarantula employs as it pads on hairy legs toward unsuspecting prey.

But because the forest is an inherently violent place, these periods of slow, careful movement are always followed by explosive bursts of speed. The tree, after many years, creaks and tumbles to a crashing demise. The creeper vine, triggered by contact, snaps reflexively inward, undoing weeks of careful growth in a ravenous instant. The tarantula strikes so fast and suddenly that it appears to teleport.

Li saw the iguana first. It crept over a fallen branch, spines standing up along its back, red eyes narrowed. In its mouth, which hung open a few degrees, triangular teeth bristled.

Dr. Alvarez and I only noticed the iguana when Li opened fire. It bulled past us, tail slicing the air and knocking Dr. Alvarez off her feet. The iguana closed the distance before Li could react. A swing of its heavy head— it didn't dare open its mouth under the hail of bullets— sent her flying with a rib-cracking thump. The SCAR skittered to a stop near the antlion pit.

Li hit a tree trunk and tumbled down. Across the clearing, I pulled my pistol's trigger as fast as I could, flinging rounds into the creature's scaly head. It turned to face me and I pivoted right, sliding into a patch of tangled weeds. Then the iguana was on me, tearing at the vegetation as I tried to wriggle deeper, the hot greedy breath washing over me—

There came a familiar gunpowder roar and a whistle of bullets through the reeds. I cowered, making myself as small as possible, and the iguana's breath vanished. It lumbered across the clearing toward Dr. Alvarez, who lowered the SCAR she'd picked up and ran. My heart dropped as she approached the antlion pit, the existence of which she must have forgotten in the heat of the moment. She was about to die in spectacularly gruesome fashion, and I couldn't pull my eyes away—

My breath sucked through my teeth as Dr. Alvarez took a running leap and vaulted the antlion pit, simply soared across the gap, scrabbling a bit on the far edge but making it up and out nonetheless, a nearly unbelievable act of athleticism and nerve, and then, as the iguana pursued, the antlion's titanic pincers erupted like a sick insectoid jack-in-the-box, closing around the iguana's midsection and dragging it into the pit.

As I struggled out of the weeds and Li rushed to Dr. Alvarez's side, a swarm of pillbugs came bouncing and rolling like gray-plated cannonballs out of the undergrowth. They bolted across the clearing, around and over the iguana as it spasmed and snapped its jaws and bled in tall wet spurts, and I had to dive out of the way to avoid being flattened. But before I even picked myself up, I realized things were about to get even worse, because pillbugs never moved like that unless something was chasing them, and sure enough after the pillbugs came a bowel-looseningly gigantic praying mantis, four stories tall, serrated forearms folded up near its thorax, the thorax itself like an electric-green rocket booster.

The mantis was less interested in us than the battered iguana, which had begun to emit guttural shrieks, one of its front legs dangling by a translucent strand of connective tissue as the remorseless antlion's pincers closed and opened and closed again. The mantis latched onto the iguana with razor-blade arms, and a tugging match ensued. Li and Dr. Alvarez took advantage of the distraction to grapple-gun away.

I watched the mantis and antlion fight over the iguana. With a terrific slippery tearing sound, the mantis ripped the top half of the iguana clean off, guts and blood fountaining while the head's eyes bulged, the shrieks cut short. The iguana's intact forearm continued to windmill, slapping hopelessly against the mantis, which dragged the head-and-upper-torso a few feet away and began to tear off thick strips of flesh.

Frozen by the gore, I took longer than I should have to notice a second praying mantis, this one stalking carefully toward me, feelers quivering above its head. I grapple-gunned at once, but the mantis followed, wings flaring as it scampered up the trunk. I undid the grapple as fast as I could to prepare for another jump. When I fired I knew it was too late, the mantis was too close, and I took a chance and leapt into the air, praying that my hook would latch in time. Dropping like a stone, I watched the hook close around a branch across the clearing, and slammed the button to cut the slack, transforming my downward momentum into a wild swing forward. At the lowest point in my swing, I hurtled past the iguana-devouring mantis, which lifted its head, quivering meat dangling out of its dainty mouth.

I retracted the line and rose, swinging back toward the mantises but ascending rapidly. As I passed overhead the ground erupted and a creature of truly titanic size, summoned by the chaos, emerged. It was shaped like a Komodo dragon but covered in matted black hair, and it had two ravenous, toothy mouths, stacked on top of each other, as if God had designed the thing with one mouth and slapped a second one underneath just for the hell of it. The antlion sucked its half of the iguana into the depths. The mantis with the other half ripped off one last scaly bite and fled, leaving a heap of bloody leftovers, which the hairy monster snarfed down at once. As its lower mouth chewed, the head whipped around, tracking the mantis as it retreated up a tree—my tree, as it happened. With a multivocal cry, the double-mouthed beast set off in pursuit.

I stood on a branch I'd thought was safe, once again aiming the grapple gun and preparing for an emergency leap, when the mantis skittered past me, trailing a shower of iguana bits. Before I could fire, the hairy creature was on me. The grapple gun flew from my hand and I tumbled down the length of the creature, managing to grab hold of the thick tangled hair just short of its rear haunch. Stunned, I clung to the creature's side, wrapping my arms in hair to keep from falling off because I could think of no alternative.

The creature smelled like wet dog times a million. My pack bounced crazily, threatening to tear me off and send me tumbling through open space. I squinted past tons of raging animal muscle and saw the canopy approaching fast, the mantis a few meters ahead. Then leaves and branches whipped by and I had to hide my face. Either the creature hadn't noticed me holding on or it didn't care, and either way I didn't see a whole lot of options besides sticking it out and hoping we wound up on the ground long enough for me to dismount.

With a crash and a sudden shift of momentum that

nearly flung me skyward, we crested the top of the tree. I was blinded by the sun, hot and huge against a motionless sky. In the distance, the mantis buzzed away, wings a blur as it soared above the wind-rustled canopy. The creature I rode unleashed a roar from both mouths. It clung, teetering, to the top of the tree. I heard an odd clicking sound and turned to see a flat tick bigger than me making its way through the matted landscape of fur. The tick's eyes were dull and expressionless, but its slavering mouthparts betrayed its carnivorous intentions.

I pulled out my pistol and shot the approaching tick four times in the head.

With a roar, the hairy beast reared on its perch and contorted itself to try and get a look at me. I lost my grip on the pistol. Somehow, impossibly, the tick crept closer, ruined face hanging loose. I climbed laterally away, toward the underside of the creature, but then an enormous hawk came screaming out of the sky and sank its talons into the hairy flesh mere inches from my face—

Each of its talons buried deep as a railroad spike, the hawk flapped its wings, gouging at the beast's eyes with a wicked beak. As the beast writhed and tumbled, both mouths snapping, I lost my hold. Jettisoned away from the melee, I fell through thick leaves and bounced to a bone-jarring halt against a wall of sharp twigs. Covered in gashes, including one on my neck that I prayed had missed my carotid, I woozily surveyed the place I'd landed.

It was a bird's nest, complete with eggshell fragments

and a disarray of discarded feathers.

Suddenly I understood why the hawk had picked a fight with such a gigantic foe. From the other side of the nest came three fledgling hawks, whose roundness and curious mannerisms would normally have provoked a smile and an "awww" from me, except that in this case they were large enough to regard me as an afternoon snack.

"No," I said, as the three fledglings hopped closer. "No, guys, trust me, don't even think about it."

With my grapple gun and pistol both gone, I settled for drawing one of my climbing picks, leaving my left arm free as I circled the nest.

"Don't do it," I warned the foremost fledgling.

"SKREE!"

As I climbed the lip of the nest, brandishing my climbing pick, a fledgling worked up the nerve to charge. Sensing a way out, I sidestepped and lunged onto its back as it passed. We tumbled out of the nest, ripping through leaves and branches, and then into open air, my arms wrapped around the fledgling's neck. Down we plummeted, the rushing air intensifying into a roar. The forest floor loomed.

"Come on," I screamed. "Fly!"

Screeching, the fledgling flapped its wings, and our descent slowed. No matter how it tried, the bird couldn't gain altitude with me on board, but it managed at least to flatten our trajectory, so that when we hit the ground we rolled instead of splattering.

Still, the speed at which we made impact was bone-splintering. Through the undergrowth I flew, glancing off rocks and roots, until I came to rest against a massive tree trunk.

The last thing I saw before blacking out was Li descending like an angel on her grapple gun's line, looking like she'd just witnessed a miracle and couldn't help but wonder if it wasn't all one big and elaborate trick.

23

"You're hurt," said Li.

"I'm fine," I said. "Scrapes and bruises. A few minutes to catch my breath and I'm ready to go."

Li bit through her protein bar and chewed viciously.

"We're almost there," said Dr. Alvarez, dangling her legs off the branch.

"Doc's right," I said, forcing a used car salesman's grin across my face. Everything hurt. My right shoulder throbbed in a way that implied it had popped out of its socket at some point before being jammed back in.

I was swabbing antiseptic on the gash in my neck when a sliver of something twitched in the wound. I probed with my fingers and gingerly pulled the splinter out.

It was the vaccine implant they'd injected back in training, a one-inch shard of silver material. I frowned. They'd said this would dissolve in weeks. What was it doing in my neck years later?

Under your skin, Tetris.

I hurled the splinter away.

"How many days, Doc?" asked Li.

"Two," said Dr. Alvarez. "Three at most."

Li tore off another chunk of protein bar. "You know what I just realized?"

I opted not to venture a guess. My mind ran laps around the vaccine implant. More lies. What else were they lying about?

As Li stared me down, I pulled my eyebrows up in an attempt to intensify what I hoped was a good-natured smile.

"Do you know the fact that is suddenly crystallizing for me," said Li, "as I sit here on a branch in the middle of the Pacific Forest, having this Eureka-style epiphanic moment of slow-dawning realization?"

"Would you care to inform me?"

"As I sit here, in the most dangerous place on Earth, between two woefully inadequate companions—stop, let me finish—between two *woefully* inadequate companions, one of whom has absolutely no business being here, and the other—upon whose body I struggle to find a single bruise-or-gash-free square inch of skin—who, as a result of recent events, is in possession of neither a grapple gun nor a firearm—what I begin to realize, Tetris, as you wave your hands and bulge your eyeballs in this most blatant fake outrage—what I realize is that all of this, the whole fucking Category 5 shitstorm we've landed ourselves in, is all one hundred percent your fault."

"No," I said, trying very hard to un-bulge my eyeballs.

"It's greed," said Li. "Ever since Cooper said the words 'ten million dollars,' your brain has been firmly switched off."

"No."

"Listen to yourself," she hissed, leaning close. "Just for one minute, snap out of this self-destructive spiral and consider what you're suggesting."

"I am listening to myself," I said, bandaging my neck. "Hello, me, what's that? You think we should keep going? Roger that, me, you're coming in loud and clear."

"Tetris."

Despite the guilty pleasure I derived from the proximity of Li's face, I found myself unable to meet her eyes. Instead I worked on swabbing a gash on my forearm. It stung. Everything stung.

"This isn't you, man," said Li, almost whispering. "I know you. You're smart. You're careful. You're risk-averse. I know you, Tetris, better than anybody knows you, and I know that you are not yourself right now."

"Then who am I?" I asked, watching red spiders wriggle out of holes in my arm and mill around on the surface. I scratched at them, but my fingers slid right through.

Li leaned back. She seemed deflated, no longer trying to meet my eyes.

"I don't know," she said. "But you're not you."

I closed my eyes and thought about telling her.

"Okay," I said, "the truth is, I've been having

nightmares."

Li took another bite of her protein bar. Dr. Alvarez, who had spent the past few minutes scooting closer, peered around Li's shoulder.

"I know that," said Li. "You've mentioned that five or six times now."

"They're getting worse," I said. "Like, every night. I'm stressing out. That's why I'm not myself."

Li chewed and scanned me. There. I'd told the truth. She wouldn't be able to find any trace of a lie on my face.

"But that doesn't mean we shouldn't go on," I said, trying to capitalize on the foothold of honesty I'd found. "They're just dreams, Li. We're so close. I can share Dr. Alvarez's grapple. And you know the pistol wouldn't have dented hardly anything anyway."

"We'll be careful," added Dr. Alvarez. "We can move slow. Take four days instead of two."

Li chewed and chewed.

"My God," she said at last, crumpling the empty wrapper and flinging it into space. "I can't believe I'm actually considering this."

At which point I knew the battle had been won.

The rest of the afternoon passed in a torturous muddle. It took significant willpower not to stagger. The tendons in my neck stood out like ski lift cables. Despite Dr. Alvarez's suggestion that we take it slow, Li strode ahead, muttering under her breath. When we turned in for the night, I hit my sleeping bag thinking I was far too exhausted even to dream. Instead I tossed and turned, head rattling with the same old blood-drenched nightmares.

In the morning I was too nauseous to eat, aching hunger or no. As we pushed forward, the floor sloped down, and the needles of Dr. Alvarez's various instruments wobbled. I stumbled along in the back, beset by faces in tree trunks that sneered or laughed, revealing mouths packed with canine teeth. The ringing in my ears was joined by a constant percussive throbbing. Once, I thought I saw Todd, bald from the chemo, standing on the other side of a clearing. When he vanished, a wave of sadness crashed over me.

That afternoon, a fog descended, beginning as a few wisps of gray and swiftly coalescing to a thick sheath that obscured my view of the tree-faces. At first I thought the fog was my imagination, but then Li stopped us for a quiet discussion and I realized the others saw it too.

"What the fuck is this, Doc?" asked Li. "I've never seen fog this thick."

"I don't know," whispered Dr. Alvarez. The fog reflected our voices back at us.

I tugged my pack straps tighter, probing absentmindedly at my thigh for the grip of a pistol that wasn't there.

"Well, we can't grapple out of it," said Li, peering upward for branches and finding nothing but fog.

"We might be close," said Dr. Alvarez. "The fog might be a product of the anomaly."

I watched Li breathe. Her face was illegible.

"Okay," she said. "What do we do?"

I cleared my throat. The sound echoed grotesquely.

"We go forward," I said.

The drumming had worked itself beyond my inner ear. There was no way I could hear anything sneaking up on us. As thick as the fog was, we wouldn't see a subway snake until we'd walked smack into its scaly flank.

Close together, practically touching, we edged forward. Dr. Alvarez juggled her instruments, whispering navigational suggestions in Li's ear. I focused on filling my lungs with wet-smelling air. Moisture beaded on my skin.

Finally we came to the end of the fog. Beyond lay a circular clearing with a giant hole in the middle. Fog, extending upward to the canopy, swirled around the perimeter as if butting against tall glass walls.

The drumming in my skull had ceased. Aside from the walled-off fog, everything was back to normal.

"Is this it?" asked Li quietly.

Dr. Alvarez didn't answer. Retrieving a high-powered flashlight from her pack, she padded toward the lip of the pit.

After a moment, Li and I followed. My legs were heavy. They took my full concentration to move, as in a dream. Our boots crunched explosively on the leaves.

Dr. Alvarez pointed her flashlight into the abyss. The cone of light caught dust particles floating in the air, but revealed no bottom. The darkness at the center of the pit remained unbroken.

She pointed the beam at the opposite wall and gradually tilted downward. The circle of light grew wider and wider as it descended, revealing a root-and-vine-riddled cross-section of the forest's innards. As it fell, the illuminated area grew more dim, until finally it vanished. No bottom.

Li produced her flare gun and aimed into the center of the pit. Before she fired, she looked at each of us, asking permission with her eyes.

We nodded. The air in the clearing froze, anticipatory and thick.

The flare gun coughed. I thought I saw the cylindrical wall of fog ripple in response. The hot-sputtering flare arced down, painting unnerving patterns of crimson and shadow.

Down the flare flew, a dwindling red star. It never hit bottom, just shrank and shrank, until finally it vanished altogether.

"No way," said Li, speaking for all of us. A slimy anxiety in my stomach forced me away from the edge.

"How deep?" I asked.

Dr. Alvarez scratched her head.

"Must be at least a couple of miles," she said, staring down.

I imagined falling in, plummeting for miles in unadulterated darkness. Would you pray for the pit to be bottomless, as you tumbled through the empty air? Or would a bottomless pit be even worse?

Near the top of the fog walls, tree trunks began to emerge.

"The fog's fading," I said.

Spurred on by my words, it flowed away in all directions, subsuming into the forest floor. The three of us stood, unable to breathe, staring at what its departure had revealed.

Clinging to the trees that encircled the clearing, with clusters of round black eyes bulging above grinning, toothy jaws, were at least a dozen specimens of a creature I hadn't seen since the day Junior died.

The long bodies of the dragons glistened with blue-black scales. Half-extended wings jutted as their spear-shaped skulls sniffed down at us.

They covered every angle of retreat except one. A single, obvious escape route, between two wide-spaced trees.

All sound had ceased. The dragons smiled, waiting.

Dr. Alvarez ran for the gap. Li and I followed. Behind us, a human laugh built in pitch and intensity over the heavy whump-whump of wings.

We crashed out of the clearing, Li quickly taking the lead. I hung close behind Dr. Alvarez as we vaulted a log and hit the ground at a sprint, our backpacks jumping and jostling. Here the floor was a ragged mess of branches and pitfalls. Li never glanced back. My heart pounded in my ears as I followed, bruises and tender joints forgotten.

With our pursuers close enough that we could feel the rush of air from their wings, Li took a hard left, Dr. Alvarez and I scrambling after her. We slid through a patch of razorgrass, then under a mossy overhang and into the open, where a dragon wheeled to cut us off. It shook the ground when it landed, flaunting its full wingspan. Li fired the SCAR as she ran, zig-zagging into a corridor between two fallen trees.

Down the narrow passageway we flew, dragons lighting on the trunks as we passed, jamming their snapping jaws into the gap. It was hard to tell their roars from the roars of the forest as it awakened. I could hardly hear my own frantic breathing.

Near the end of the passageway, the ground began to swell. As we leapt clear and stumbled to our feet beyond the fallen trees, a subway snake burst out of the bulge, shaking off huge clods of dirt, which thudded like mortar shells around us. Li headed toward a thick patch of undergrowth, Dr. Alvarez close behind. A dragon plummeted from the sky to our left and scrambled along the ground on all fours, mouth widening in preparation for a strike.

The subway snake hurled its Brontosaurian bulk across the clearing and clamped huge jaws around the dragon's unguarded torso. The crunch of so much raw meat colliding at such incredible speed released a shock wave that nearly knocked us off our feet. One wing trapped, the dragon flailed and shrieked, scrabbling at the snake's gigantic head.

We thrashed through the undergrowth. Probably the majority of the dragons were now occupied, but Li seemed to think it was a good idea to put more distance between us and them before risking a grapple. My ankles emitted white shrapnel-bursts of pain as I fought across the weed-strewn ground.

Beyond the thick vegetation, we found ourselves before a chasm bridged by a fallen tree. Li wasted no time scurrying across, arms extended for balance. Dr. Alvarez and I followed.

Midway across, my foot plunged into a soft pit of decayed wood, and I tripped. Picking myself up, I felt a whoosh of air and snapped around to glimpse the descending shape of a dragon. With a sickening crack, the dragon landed on the bridge behind me. Li's SCAR roared, but the sound was lost in the splintering of the dead tree's core. At first the bridge sagged mildly, and I thought for a moment it would hold, but then the dragon stepped clumsily about, shrieking as it tried to maintain its balance, and the whole bug-eaten tree crunched downward beneath its feet—

Wishing like hell for the grapple gun I didn't have, I caught a glimpse of Li and Dr. Alvarez staring down from the edge of the chasm, above me now as I scrambled up the crazily-leaning trunk, and then the dragon took off, kicking the two tree-halves downward, my stomach leaping against my throat, and I fell, unbelieving, into bottomless darkness.

24

Up on the wall of the Hawaiian fortress, leaning on the parapet a few dozen meters from the gate, stood Lindsey Li. She wore sunglasses and stared across the stump-scarred no-man's-land into the jungle. Every once in a while she worked up enough spittle to fire a glob over the edge.

The soldiers on watch had learned to leave her alone. Trying to engage her in conversation provoked an emotionless stare that screamed "not-to-be-fucked-with." Privately she was the subject of much discussion, standing up there as she did in the same spot every day. Her companions—the weaselly agency guy and the academic chick who'd known her way around a machine gun—had returned to the mainland a few days back. But this one, the first female ranger any of them had ever seen, had stayed behind.

Li wasn't sure why she'd stayed. She knew Tetris was dead. She and Dr. Alvarez had circled back after the chaos died down and taken a look in the chasm where he'd fallen. Hadn't found anything except spiders, which had chased them right out of there. She felt no doubt whatsoever. So why did she keep coming out here?

Guilt, probably. She felt guilty. Because if she'd asserted herself, really refused to take "no" for an answer, they would have turned around, and Tetris wouldn't have died. All that shit she gave him for being greedy, and in the end it turned out she was just as greedy as he was.

Not for the money. It was the mystery that called to her, the desire to understand. So she'd held her tongue and let Tetris goad them on, and what had they found?

A hole in the ground.

That was it. That was what Tetris had died for: an abnormally deep ravine.

She spat and watched the globe of spittle wobble and spread until it was too small to see.

******

I regained consciousness in total darkness. Waking

took several minutes, and at first I didn't realize what was happening, only that the darkness was changing somehow, gliding over itself on well-oiled rails. I had a sense that something lurked behind a thick black curtain in front of me.

It was quiet. Dead, dull, deep-buried silence. I thought I heard a trickling, some faraway subterranean stream.

Was I dead?

I lay on a bed of soft material. Moss, maybe. It was cool against my neck. I found that I could work my fingers into it, through tightly knit, fine-leafed vegetable matter that sprang back into place when my fingers retreated.

The moss held water like a sponge. As I felt around, dew transferred in fine drops to my skin. I lifted some of the moisture to my mouth, expecting the clear taste of a quick-running mountain stream, but tasted only my grimy fingers.

Slowly, as the murk of sleep faded away, I discovered that the lower half of my body had vanished. I felt at my legs. They were still attached. I couldn't feel them, though, even when I prodded and pinched the skin through my pants. I slid my hands along my thighs, the flesh dead and silent beneath my fingertips. Then, right above my hips, I felt sensation return.

Touching my lower back provoked a spike of white pain so intense that I nearly bit through my tongue trying to keep from crying out. My hand came away drenched with blood. I wrenched myself up on my elbows and tugged my heavy legs into a sitting position. Groping in the dark, gasping from the pain, I found a mossy slope—a root, maybe. I dragged myself closer.

Leaning against the slope, I closed my eyes and tried to distract myself by taking an inventory of what I'd lost.

My pack: gone. Grapple gun and pistol: both gone. Gone, too, were my legs, and with them any hope of survival.

Li and Dr. Alvarez were gone. I'd never see them again. Neither would I see Zip, or my dad, with whom I would never have a chance to make amends. I'd never get a chance to track my mother down.

The whole hopeful narrative of the life I'd planned began to shudder and crumble before me. Why?

I began to cry.

I stifled the sound at first, but the sobs bubbled up out of my chest with too much force. Then I realized I didn't care if some monster found me, I was dead no matter what, and I stopped holding back.

I hoped Li and Dr. Alvarez had continued running instead of trying to save me. They probably hadn't. Which meant I had killed three people instead of one. And it had been me who killed us. How many warnings had I ignored? How many chances had I thrown away? I'd imagined myself to be invincible. That seemed obvious, now. The ultimate arrogance. Other rangers died; I could accept this fact. But not me. I was different. I was smarter, quicker, guarded by luck.

But the forest knew better. The forest had laughed at my arrogance and snapped my spine like a Popsicle stick.

I shouted something beyond comprehension. My voice plowed into the mossy walls and died. I sucked in air and screamed, no words, just a furious animal cry, trailing off only when my lungs deflated completely. Again I screamed, and again, and then out of the darkness came an enormous grasping claw, wrapping itself around my head, and a voice beside my ear breathed a single word:

TETRIS.

I flailed, trying to wrench myself free, but the grip on my skull was far too firm, and at once I was bound on all sides, crushed inward, unable to shout, hardly able even to breathe, and it was only my eyes that could move, rolling in their sockets as I strained to see something, anything, of the creature that now possessed me.

TETRIS, said the voice, in my other ear this time.

"What are you?" I gasped, and suddenly it became excruciatingly bright. I had to screw my eyes shut to keep from being blinded, and when I peeled them open, I was in a room with shining white walls. I sat, immobilized by invisible restraints, atop a wicker chair, across the table from a flickering image of Junior.

"Junior?" I said, the horror of the earliest dreams returning in full force.

NOT JUNIOR, whisperscreamed the voice, as Junior inclined his head, eyes flickering from normal to shiny and back again. His mouth remained clamped shut.

"You're it," I said. "You're what lives in the forest."

The image flickered, bathing Junior head to toe in blood.

NOT LIVE. INCORRECT NOT LIVE. AM. AM AM AM AM AM.

Now the voice came from inside me, somehow, resonating in my bones.

"I don't understand," I said.

SHOW, THEN, said the voice, and an image slammed across my view.

I saw the Earth, the ocean-Earth with all its glittering blue. It floated like a jewel in boundless starry space. I sat atop a huge, round, cavernous rock, and watched the Earth grow before me. Deep in the asteroid, I saw/felt a seed, a kernel, a core, a not-quite embryo. And as the asteroid plunged into the atmosphere, I saw that the continents were foreign, somehow, clumped together, and I understood that this was not some alternate reality, this was Earth, the real Earth, my Earth, before the forest, sixty-five million years ago.

And then the asteroid flung hunks of plasma as the ravenous atmosphere tore at its skin, and inside I felt the seed/kernel/embryo stir, not grasp what was happening, precisely, but feel in some deep instinctual place that it was time, that life was near, and then the asteroid hit the planet and was obliterated, and I was obliterated, and the Earth was obliterated, great banks of dust rising above the shaking ground and filling the prehistorically starry sky.

Time jumped, and I shrank to the size of a virus, deep in the ocean beside the towering embryo from the asteroid's core, and I watched as molecules began to pull apart around me, as atoms, even, bared their neutrons and protons, stimulated somehow by the embryo, electrons zipping around in panic. I felt a sensation of zooming, time quickening, and my field of view changed. The embryo grew, adding to itself exponentially, tearing apart matter in a bubbling frenzy and glomping freshly-minted molecules onto extensions of itself, on every edge, every fractally-divergent extremity sucking in water as the organism grew and grew and grew and grew, and then, as time quickened further, millenia flashing past, the oceans dwindled and the forest spread, and I finally began to understand.

"You *are* the forest," I said, and the image vanished. I sat across the table from Junior, who smiled, revealing teeth that changed as frequently as his eyes, first clean and white, then bloodied, then sharp and multi-peaked like a piranha's.

AM FOREST. AM AM AM.

"The nightmares," I said, "the hallucinations—you sent those?"

YES.

I gritted my chipped and aching teeth. "Why? Why torture me?"

NOT INTENDED. NOT NIGHTMARES NO JUST MESSAGES. MESSAGES FILTERED POLLUTED TWISTED BY TINY PRIMITIVE HUMAN MIND, HUMAN BRAIN WITH PRIMITIVE PSYCHIC RECEPTORS VERY FAR, FAR FAR FAR VERY FAR AWAY.

I looked at Junior, focused on him. Found that, with a

bit of concentration, I could stabilize his appearance.

"You were trying to communicate," I said.

YES.

"But I never got anything out of those dreams. That's all I thought they were. Dreams."

HAD TO BRING—HAD TO BRING A HUMAN. HAD TO BRING YOU.

"That's what the obelisk was? What the tablet was? What Roy LaMonte saw? All to bring someone here?"

YES. YES YES YES.

"Could have just sent a letter," I said. "Seems like that ought to be within the capabilities of a giant sentient forest."

Without warning, I found myself staring at another image of the globe, this time the familiar Earth with forests instead of oceans.

SIXTY-FIVE MILLION YEARS OF LIFE.

I watched sixty-five million years whip by in thirty seconds, the continents gliding and morphing into their familiar shapes.

THEN—HUMANS.

And I watched as humans appeared, spread across the whole planet, built factories and extinguished ecosystems and, finally, began to probe in earnest at the borders of the forest. I felt the forest's curiosity, its confusion... and, beneath it all, an unmistakable tinge of fear.

SIXTY-FIVE MILLION YEARS OF FOREST. TEN THOUSAND YEARS OF THIS.

Images whipped by: primitive humans perfecting fire.

The first airships floating over the canopy. Wars on the continents, hundreds of thousands of deaths in the trenches, blood and gunpowder and screams both verbal and psychic, and then the biggest, brightest scream of them all, a flash of light over Hiroshima, and then, before the first shock had faded, again at Nagasaki—

Here the image froze. The view rotated, swiveling around the blooming mushroom cloud with its impossibly bright point of origin, and through the image it was somehow relayed to me how the forest had felt at that moment, watching the cloud rise, seeing, finally, after sixty-five million years, the birth of a terrestrial force that had the capacity to cause it harm.

DO YOU SEE? asked the forest.

"I see," I said.

The forest brooded.

NEED TO KNOW, it said, IF HUMANS CAN BE TRUSTED.

I snorted. "And that's why you brought me? To probe in my brain, figure out whether you could trust me? What happens if you decide you can't?"

A flurry of images, a million swollen bulbs, lurking in the canopy all around the globe, filled to near-bursting with what I understood wordlessly to be an incredibly potent neurotoxin.

"You're going to kill us," I said. "You're going to flood the air and kill us all."

NO, said the forest. DO NOT WANT TO.

The image vanished, the white room vanished, and I

found myself back in darkness, still encapsulated by what I now recognized as a form-fitting cage of throbbing plant matter.

BUT, said the forest, MIGHT HAVE TO.

"Why?"

BECAUSE OF THIRTY THOUSAND NUCLEAR WARHEADS POINTED AT MY NEUROLOGICAL CENTERS.

For some reason this struck me as hilarious. Perhaps I'd lost enough blood to drive me to delirium, but either way I couldn't stop my chest from shaking. I tried to put my finger on what I found so funny, and eventually it occurred to me:

"Cooper said we couldn't let you know that we knew you existed," I said. "And now you're saying that you yourself are afraid to let them know that you already know that they know that you exist?"

Silence.

CORRECT.

"Why can't we just tell each other outright? Why this skulking in shadows?"

IF EACH ACTOR HAS THE POWER TO DESTROY THE OTHER, WITH NO CHANCE OF REPRISAL, AND BOTH ACTORS UNDERSTAND THIS FACT, A PREEMPTIVE STRIKE IS THE MOST STRATEGICALLY SOUND DECISION.

I scrunched my eyebrows together. The volume of the voice had decreased significantly, while the messages themselves had grown more complex. As if the forest was calibrating to my mind.

"I don't understand," I said. "In that case, why haven't you already killed us off?"

The silence stretched on so long that I began to think it had forgotten about me.

BECAUSE, said the forest, its tone somehow reluctant, I MAY NEED YOUR HELP.

It showed me another image of the modern-day Earth. Then the view swiveled, away from the planet and out into empty, star-speckled space.

SOMETHING IS COMING, said the forest. SOMETHING FROM FAR AWAY. COMING FAST. SEVEN REVOLUTIONS, PERHAPS, BEFORE IT ARRIVES.

The stars vanished.

"What is it?" I asked.

DO NOT KNOW. BUT FEEL IT COMING, AND FEEL... MALICE. HUNGER TEETH MERCILESS APPETITE DARK RAVENING HUNGER.

I shivered, although the air down here was warm, almost too warm. My skin pearled with sweat.

"And you want our help with it, whatever it is."

IN SEVEN REVOLUTIONS, CAN ONLY DO SO MUCH. NEED DECADES CENTURIES MILLENIA TO PREPARE. BUT WITH HUMANS, IN SEVEN REVOLUTIONS—WITH MY HELP—

Silence, again, as the forest either absorbed itself in thought or waited for my response.

"I have so many questions," I said.

ASK.

"If you wanted us to get here so bad, why not clear the monsters out of our way?"

The forest, amused: LIKE ASKING A HUMAN TO KEEP WHITE BLOOD CELLS FROM ATTACKING BACTERIA.

"Why did you stop at the coasts? Why not grow over the entire planet?"

LIKE ASKING A FIT HUMAN WHY DID HE NOT GROW TO BE FOUR HUNDRED POUNDS WHEN HE HAD ACCESS TO THE REQUISITE NUTRIENTS.

I chewed at loose skin on my lips. The pain in my back had only grown worse.

"Well," I said, feeling gloomy again, "I don't think I can help you explain things to the rest of the humans. My back's broken. I'm bleeding to death."

For a long time, I sat in my cage, listening to the burble of the faraway stream, waiting for a reply.

The forest had abandoned me. Either it had already learned everything it wanted to know, or it had no use for a human without functioning legs. Both options were equally depressing.

God, I didn't want to die. I pressed a hand against the wound on my lower back and felt the lifeblood seeping out. This was how I was going to go, huh? Meek and silent, buried deep underground, accepting my fate without a fight?

"Hey," I shouted, my voice hoarse. "Hey, is that it? You leaving me to die?"

Still the silence dragged on. I strained against the bonds, then gave up, counting heartbeats in my aching temples.

Something stirred in the darkness.

IT MAY BE POSSIBLE TO FIX YOU, said the forest at last. BUT THERE WILL BE A COST.

A thrill of hope shivered up my spine. I licked my ruptured lips.

"If it saves my life, I'll pay any price," I said.

There was definitely a stream in the distance, trickling endlessly onward.

LIKEWISE, said the forest, as tendrils plunged into my lower back, my spine, and the back of my skull, unthinkable white-hot pain slamming me unconscious.

*****

Once, in first or second grade, Li had just about burned her house down trying to bake a cake. She still had nightmares about the egg-draped, icing-smeared kitchen, flames billowing out of the oven. Had stuck around to try and put it out and barely made it out in time. When the firefighters arrived, she was trying to get the neighbor's garden hose to reach the crackling inferno. Years later, she retained a deep aversion to cooking.

"I can't believe my eyes," her mom had said when she made it back from work and saw the wreckage.

That stupid cliché had been bouncing around Li's head ever since. But she never really understood what it meant, until one morning on the ramparts of the Hawaiian base, when someone who looked an awful lot like Tetris came strolling out of the jungle, arms swinging empty-handed at his sides.

And if she closed her eyes at first, and rubbed her sunglasses on her shirt, and had to take a second look to be sure, she could have been forgiven, because, sunglasses or no, her eyes reported that Tetris's swinging arms, and the skin of his faintly smiling face, were tinged the unmistakable light-green tone of upper-canopy leaves.

About the Author

Justin Groot lives in Southern California, where he spends most of his free time reading, writing, playing videogames, and rock climbing.

Twitter: @JustinGroot3

Made in the USA
Middletown, DE
30 July 2019